跟莎士比亞
一學就會的
1000單字

—— 黎弼芳 / 著 ——

1000 Vocabulary of Shakespeare's Dramas

國家圖書館出版品預行編目資料

跟莎士比亞一學就會的1000單字 /
黎弼芳著. -- 初版. -- 新北市 : 雅典文化, 民105.08
　面 ；　公分. -- （英語工具書 ； 10）
　　ISBN 978-986-5753-69-6(平裝)

1. 英語　2. 詞彙

805.12　　　　　　　　　　　105009920

英語工具書系列　10

跟莎士比亞一學就會的1000單字

著／黎弼芳
責任編輯／李淑芳
內文排版／王國卿
封面設計／姚恩涵

法律顧問：方圓法律事務所／涂成樞律師

總經銷：永續圖書有限公司　　CVS代理／美璟文化有限公司

永續圖書線上購物網　　TEL：（02）2723-9968
www.foreverbooks.com.tw　　FAX：（02）2723-9668

出版日／2016年8月

 雅典文化

出版社　22103　　新北市汐止區大同路三段194號9樓之1
　　　　　　TEL　（02）8647-3663
　　　　　　FAX˙（02）8647-3660

〈前言〉

英語學習是種終身學習，而且只要你不停止學習，就能夠在持續進步中，漸漸發現學習英語的無窮樂趣和無限可能，因為學習不會也不應該只有一種方法。

為什麼學莎士比亞

單字要會用的才是你的

我們都知道單字是英語聽說讀寫能力的基礎，認識愈多單字就愈有益於全方位提昇英語能力，不過單字量的建立必須花時間去累積，不太容易一蹴即成，此外還要有廣泛學習的態度，千萬不要偏廢某類單字，更不應該認為簡單的單字不值得學習，事實上，單字沒有所謂的難易問題，重點在於你能不能用出來，單字要會用的才是你的，才真的是學會了。假如你願意花點時間去注意的話，就不難發現許多口譯員在做中翻英時所使用的單字，其實並不難，大都是口語常用的字，當然這絕對跟英語程度無關，而是他們懂得如何靈活運用簡單的單字，來表達豐富的意思。

態度歸零，多元英語學習

英語世界傳世的文學作品，除了探討人生與人性，

更蘊含文學和語言之美，無疑是學習英語的優良教材，適合每一個對英語有興趣的學習者，不應該只是文學院的教材，尤其是一些家喻戶曉的文學作品，更值得我們以學習英語的角度去親近和認識。

莎士比亞（William Shakespeare，1564-1616）是英國文藝復興時期的戲劇家和詩人，早期創作了一些詩歌，但主要作品是戲劇，其戲劇作品是至今沒有其他英語戲劇能夠超越的鉅作，現存的劇本共有37部。

根據語言學家研究統計，莎士比亞的所有戲劇所使用的單字約15000字，不過莎士比亞那個年代的一般人，卻大概只有300字的單字量；當時受過大學高等教育、能夠閱讀《聖經》和《莎士比亞》的人，在與人對話時會出現的單字量，大約是 3000 到 4000 字，而口才很好的人，則在一萬左右的單字量。不過由於莎士比亞會自行造字，因此，根據統計，他劇本裡出現過兩次的單字不超過5000字。

由於莎士比亞時期的英語是近代英語，其語法和拼寫不像現代已經標準化了，因而與現代人所使用的英語有許多出入，所以，本書從莎士比亞四大悲劇以及四大喜劇精選出1000個句子，並配合原句列出符合現代英語語法的譯句，幫助讀者讀懂莎士比亞的句子，讓你在欣賞莎士比亞戲劇句子的同時，結合譯句增加學習的記憶點，使書中所列現代英語中常用的單字、片語和短語，深刻在你的腦海中，進而自然而然在聽說讀寫時運用出

來。本書收錄的四大悲劇包括《哈姆雷特》（Hamlet）、《李爾王》（King Lear）、《麥克白》（Macbeth）、《奧賽羅》（Othello）；四大喜劇包括《無事自擾》（Much Ado About Nothing）、《仲夏夜之夢》（A Midsummer Night's Dream）、《威尼斯商人》（The Merchant of Venice）、《第十二夜》（Twelfth night）。

　　依循不同的估算方法，今日的英語單字有一說是一百萬字，另一說是十億字，儘管在莎士比亞那個時代，5000個單字已經很不錯，但若與現在的單字量相比，5000個單字不能算多，甚至還只是學習英語單字的基礎量。以目前台灣的學生而言，大學入學考試中心所公佈的單字就有7,000個。事實上，學習單字無須貪多，重點是能夠運用，如果為了應付考試，硬是背下7,000個單字，考完就忘記了，這樣的學習方法不但痛苦且英語能力的提昇有限。所以，希望你從現在開始以歸零的態度，善用各式各樣的教材來學習英語，本書就是你的好選擇，陪伴你透過莎士比亞的戲劇，無痛學會1000個好用的單字、片語和短語，不但能夠開創英語學習樂趣，更是提升學習效率的全新體驗。

莎士比亞生平與創作

平凡中有不平凡

莎士比亞於1564年4月23日出生於英格蘭沃里克郡

雅芳河畔的斯特拉特福（Stratford-upon-Avon），展開了他總是在平凡中透著不平凡的生命歷程。他的父親約翰莎士比亞（John Shakespeare），是一個手套商人和市參議員，母親瑪麗阿登（Mary Arden）是一位富裕地主的女兒。莎士比亞在鎮上的國王學校受教育，18 歲時與安妮哈瑟維（Anne Hathaway）結婚，婚後育有三個孩子：大女兒和龍鳳胎的雙胞胎。

行蹤成謎的歲月

莎士比亞開始創作的確切時間至今仍然是個謎，但根據記錄顯示，到 1592 年為止，他在倫敦已極具知名度，倫敦舞台也表演了他的幾部劇作。不過他在 1585 年到 1592 年之間卻行蹤成謎，許多傳記作者描述很多虛構故事試圖說明他這段時期的經歷，學者則稱這段時間為莎士比亞「行蹤成謎的歲月」（lost years）。

最後的直系後代

莎士比亞於 1616 年 4 月 23 日逝世，留下了妻子和兩個女兒。大女兒蘇珊娜和內科醫生約翰霍爾於 1607 年結婚，二女兒裘蒂絲在莎士比亞逝世前兩個月嫁給酒商托馬斯基內爾。他在遺囑中，將大量地產的大部分留給大女兒，同時指定她將財產原封不動地傳給她的第一個兒子。二女兒一家有三個孩子，但都還沒有結婚就去世了。大女兒有一個女兒伊莉莎白，她結了兩次婚，但是 1670 年去世時沒有留下一個孩子，莎士比亞的直系後代即到

此為止。

舊題材注入新生命

莎士比亞現存的劇本共三十七部，多取材於歷史、小說、民間傳說和老戲目等已有的材料，但在改寫中注入了自己的想法，給舊題材賦予新穎、豐富、深刻的內容。他一方面廣泛借鑑古代戲劇、英國中世紀戲劇以及歐洲新興的文化藝術；一方面深刻觀察人生，瞭解社會，掌握時代的脈搏，藉此反映封建社會向資本主義社會過渡的歷史現實，宣揚新興中產階級的人道主義思想和人性論觀點，塑造了眾多栩栩如生的人物形象。

新悲劇角色

莎士比亞的悲劇標示著他對時代、人生的深入思考，他塑造的新時代悲劇主角從中世紀的禁錮和蒙昧中醒來，在象徵近代的黎明照耀下，雄心勃勃地想要發展或完善自己，但又無法克服時代和自身的局限，終於在環境和內心的矛盾掙扎中，遭到不可避免的失敗和犧牲。例如：哈姆雷特為父報仇就是因為發現時代不同了，他決定要擔起重整的責任，結果是空懷大志，無力回天。

喜劇爭取自由幸福

莎士比亞的喜劇大都以愛情、友誼、婚姻為主題，主要角色多是一些具有人文主義智慧與美德的青年男女。莎士比亞透過這些角色爭取自由、幸福，並歌頌進步、

美好的新時代，他溫和地揭露和嘲諷舊事物的衰朽和醜惡，如禁欲主義的虛矯、清教徒的偽善和高利貸者的貪鄙等。

戲劇替自然照鏡子

莎士比亞認為，戲劇彷彿要給自然照一照鏡子，讓德行看一看自己的面貌，使荒唐瞧一瞧自己的姿態，給時代和社會認清自己的形象和印記。他的作品從真實生活出發，深刻地反映時代的風貌和社會的本質。哲學家馬克思、恩格斯將莎士比亞推崇為現實主義的經典作家，提出戲劇創作應該更加「莎士比亞化」。

時代的傳聲筒

莎士比亞戲劇的特點：善於從真實生活出發，展示廣闊的社會背景，給作品中的人物和事件提供富有時代特色的典型環境，是時代的傳聲筒；情節生動、豐富；人物個性鮮明，同時具有典型意義；巧妙結合現實主義的刻畫和浪漫主義的氛圍；語言富麗，富表現力；作家的意向透過情節和人物的描述自然地流露出來。

《馬克白》（*Macbeth*）

Part 2. 四大喜劇

《威尼斯商人》（*The Merchant of Venice*） 177

《仲夏夜之夢》（*A Midsummer Night's Dream*） 215

《無事自擾》（*Much Ado About Nothing*） 249

《第十二夜》 (*Twelfth Night*) 283

Part 1.

四大悲劇

《哈姆雷特》
(Hamlet)

　　哈姆雷特（Hamlet）是丹麥王國一位年輕有為的王子，他正在德國學習時，國內傳來父王突然慘死的噩耗，叔叔克勞迪斯（Claudius）篡奪王位，母親歌楚德（Gertrude）改嫁克勞迪斯。

　　哈姆雷特回國奔喪，在一天深夜，他在城堡裡見到父親的鬼魂，父親的鬼魂告訴他自己被害的經過，原來是克勞迪斯趁老哈姆雷特（指哈姆雷特的父親）在花園裡午睡時，把致命的毒液滴進了他的耳朵，奪取了他的生命。老哈姆雷特要求兒子為他報仇，但不許傷害他的母親，要讓她受到良心的譴責。哈姆雷特知道真相後，變得精神恍惚，整天穿著黑色喪服，一心想著復仇。

　　有一天，他去見自己的戀人，也就是首相普羅尼斯（Polonius）的女兒奧菲麗雅（Ophelia），但復仇使得他心神不寧，因而行為變得十分怪誕。奧菲麗雅把王子的情況告訴首相，首相又報告了克勞迪斯。克勞迪斯雖然

不知道老國王鬼魂出現的事，但他心中有鬼，便派人試探哈姆雷特。哈姆雷特一方面想復仇，一方面又礙於母親的面子，同時又無法十分確定父親鬼魂的話，因而深陷苦惱中。

後來，哈姆雷特決心要設法證實克勞斯迪的罪行，正好宮中來了一個戲團，他便安排他們演出一齣戲，內容與老哈姆雷特在花園遇害的情節相同。演出時，哈姆雷特在旁邊仔細觀察克勞迪斯，只見他坐立不安，中途就離去，於是哈姆雷特確認了父親鬼魂的話，決定復仇。

接下來有一天，哈姆雷特恰巧看見克勞迪斯獨自在懺悔，他本來可以殺死他，卻又覺得懺悔中的人被殺後會進入天堂，因而作罷了。克勞迪斯派王后勸說哈姆雷特，哈姆雷特與母親發生爭執，誤殺躲在幃幕後偷聽的首相。克勞迪斯以首相的兒子雷歐提斯（Laertes）要為父親報仇為由，要將哈姆雷特送往英國，準備借英王之手除掉哈姆雷特。哈姆雷特識破克勞迪斯的詭計，中途返回丹麥。這時，奧菲麗雅受刺激發瘋，最後落水身亡，哈姆雷特回國時，正好趕上她的葬禮。緊接著，克勞迪斯挑撥奧菲麗雅的哥哥雷歐提斯和哈姆雷特決鬥，並在暗中準備毒劍和毒酒要殺害哈姆雷特。

哈姆雷特在第一會合獲勝，克勞迪斯假意祝賀送上毒酒，但哈姆雷特沒喝。哈姆雷特第二回合獲勝，王后一高興，喝下去原來準備給哈姆雷特的毒酒。決鬥中，哈姆雷特誤中了毒劍，他奪過劍後也擊中了雷歐提斯。

王后中毒死去，雷歐提斯也在生命的最後一刻揭露了克
勞迪斯的陰謀。哈姆雷特用盡最後的力氣以手中的毒劍
擊中克勞迪斯，自己也毒發自亡。

---

001. there *(adv.)* 在那裡

英文 Who's there?

原句 *Who's there?*

中文 誰在那裡？

---

002. right on time *(ph.)* 準時

英文 You are right on time.

原句 *You come most carefully upon your hour.*

中文 你準時來了。

---

003. nothing *(pron.), (n.)* 沒事，沒什麼

英文 I have seen nothing.

原句 *I have seen nothing.*

中文 我什麼也沒看見。

---

004. torment *(vt.)* 使痛苦，糾纏

英文 It torments me with fear and wonder.

原句 *It harrows me with fear and wonder.*

中文 它以恐懼和疑惑使我感到痛苦。

---

005. fantasy *(n.)* 幻想，想像，空想

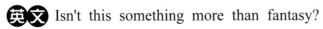 Isn't this something more than fantasy?

 *Is not this something more than fantasy?*

 這樣還只是幻想嗎？

●track *002*

---

006. doubt *(vt.)* , *(vi.)* , *(n.)* 懷疑，疑慮

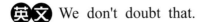 We don't doubt that.

We doubt it nothing.

我們沒有懷疑那件事。

---

007. offence *(n.)* 冒犯，犯罪，罪過

It's an offence against heaven.

'Tis a fault to heaven.

這是對上天不敬。

---

008. frailty *(n.)* 脆弱，虛弱

Frailty, your name is women!

Frailty, thy name is woman!

脆弱，你的名字是女人。

---

009. hold my tongue *(ph.)* 保持沉默

英文 I had to hold my tongue.

原句 *I must hold my tongue.*

中文 我必須保持沉默。

---

010. glad *(adj.)* 高興的，樂意的

英文 I am very glad to see you.

原句 *I am very glad to see you.*

中文 我非常高興看到你。

---

011. strange *(adj.)* 奇怪的，陌生的，不可思議的；
(adv.) 奇怪地，外行地

英文 It's very strange.

原句 *'Tis very strange.*

中文 這很奇怪！

---

012. reward *(vt.)*, *(n.)* 報答，獎賞

英文 I'll reward you.

原句 *I will requite your loves.*

中文 我會報答你。

被引用最多的莎劇

　　《哈姆雷特》又名《王子復仇記》，是莎士比亞於 1599 年至 1602 年間創作的悲劇作品，是他最負盛名和被人引用最多的劇本，似乎不停地被他人講述、改編著，同時也是莎劇中最長的一齣。劇中叔叔謀害了國王，篡奪王位，並娶了國王的遺孀；王子哈姆雷特因此為父王向叔叔報復。劇本細緻地刻畫了偽裝的和真實的瘋癲，以及從悲痛欲絕到假裝憤怒的人生境遇，探索了背叛、復仇、亂倫、墮落等主題。

●track *003*

---

013. affection *(n.)* 愛，情愛

英文 Keep you in the rear of your affection.

原句 *Keep you in the rear of your affection.*

中文 不要表露出你的感情。

---

014. unmask *(vt.)* , *(vi.)* 揭露，揭下……假面具

英文 She unmask her beauty to the moon.

原句 *She unmask her beauty to the moon.*

中文 她對著月亮展露她的美麗。

---

015. **thorny** *(adj.)* 多刺的，長滿荊棘的，棘手的

英文 Show me the steep and thorny way to heaven.

原句 *Show me the steep and thorny way to heaven.*

中文 指示我到達天堂那條陡峭且長滿荊棘的路。

---

016. **remind** *(vt.)* 提醒，使想起

英文 That reminds me.

原句 *'Tis told me,*

中文 這提醒我了。

● track *004*

---

017. **custom** *(n.)* 習俗，慣例，習慣

英文 Is it a local custom?

原句 *Is it a custom?*

中文 這是本地習俗嗎？

---

018. **call** *(vt.)* , *(vi.)* 叫喊，呼喚，把……叫作；
(n.) 呼叫，訪問

英文 I'll call you Hamlet.

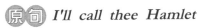 *I'll call thee Hamlet*

中文 我會叫你哈姆雷特。

019. hands off *(ph.)* 把手放開，不干涉

英文 Get your hands off me.

原句 *Hold off your hands.*

中文 把你的手放開。

020. destiny *(n.)* 命運

英文 My destiny is calling.

原句 *My fate cries out.*

中文 我的命運在呼喚著。

● track *005*

021. further *(adj.)* 更遠的，更進一步的；
(adv.) 更遠地，更深一層地

英文 I won't go any further.

原句 *I'll go no further.*

中文 我不要再前進了。

022. revenge *(vt.)* 替……報仇；*(n.)* 報仇，報復

英文 Take revenge for his horrible murder, that crime against

nature.

原句 *Revenge his foul and most unnatural murder.*

中文 你必須為他報仇，因為他被慘忍地殺害了。

023. at least *(ph.)* 至少，無論如何

英文 That was at least certain in Denmark.

原句 *At least I'm sure it may be so in Denmark*

中文 至少在丹麥是如此。

024. sworn (swear 的過去分詞) *(vt.)* 使宣誓；
(vi.) 發誓，詛咒

英文 I have sworn it.

原句 *I have sworn't.*

中文 我已經發誓了。

025. grave *(vt.)* 雕刻；*(n.)* 墓穴

英文 It doesn't need a ghost, come from the grave, to tell us that.

原句 *There needs no ghost, my lord, come from the grave, to tell us this.*

中文 這件事不需要鬼從墳墓裡出來告訴我們，大家也能明白。

●track *006*

---

026. intend *(vt.)* 想要，打算

英文 I intended to do that.

原句 *I did intend it.*

中文 我打算過要這樣做。

---

027. far *(adj.)* 遠的，較遠的；*(adv.)* 遙遠地，極；
(n.) 遠方

英文 You may go that far.

原句 *You may go so far.*

中文 你可以處理 (做) 到那個程度。

---

028. accuse *(vt.)* 指控，譴責，指責，歸咎 (於)

英文 You mustn't accuse him of anything really bad.

原句 *You must not put another scandal on him.*

中文 你不可以真的指責他有任何的不好。

---

029. bait *(vt.)* 引誘，置餌於；*(n.)* 誘餌，圈套

英文 Your bait of falsehood catches the big carp of truth.

原句 *Your bait of falsehood takes this carp of truth.*

中文 你大膽假設的誘餌釣到了象徵真相的大鯉魚。

030. get it *(ph.)* 懂得，瞭解

英文 Have you got it?

原句 *You have me, have you not?*

中文 你懂我的意思嗎？

031. matter *(vi.)* 有關係，要緊事情；*(n.)* 問題，事態，重要性，物質

英文 What's the matter?

原句 *What's the matter?*

中文 怎麼了？

032. piteous *(adj.)* 可憐的，淒慘的

033. expression *(n.)* 表達，表情，措辭

英文 He had such a piteous expression, as though he had been released from hell to tell us of its horrors.

原句 *As if he had been loosed out of hell, to speak of horrors—he comes before me.*

中文 他的表情很可憐，好像從地獄被放出來訴說著嚇人的事情。

　　《哈姆雷特》有三個早期版本，版本之間存在著一些不同的內文、甚至是整段劇幕，戲劇的結構以及角色的深度也吸引評論家的注意。例如：哈姆雷特刺殺叔叔時的遲疑，這個辯論長達幾個世紀，有些人認為這不過是戲劇拖延的手法，但另一些人則認為它是哲學與道德的問題，討論了冷血謀殺、精密復仇、欲望受挫的矛盾。

●track *007*

034.　transformation *(n.)* 變化，轉變，變形

英文 I suppose you've heard about the transformation that's taken place in Hamlet.

原句 *Something have you heard of Hamlet's "transformation".*

中文 我猜想你們已經聽說了哈姆雷特的轉變 (這裡指他瘋了)。

035. a great deal *(ph.)* 很多，大量

英文 He's talked about you a great deal.

原句 *He hath much talk'd of you.*

中文 他經常談起你們。

036. be happy with *(ph.)* 滿足的，滿意的

英文 We're happy with that.

原句 *It likes us well.*

中文 我們很滿意。

037. brevity *(n.)* 簡潔，簡練，(時間等的) 短暫

英文 Brevity is the soul of wit.

原句 *Brevity is the soul of wit*

中文 簡潔是智慧的靈魂。

038. ardently *(adv.)* 熱心地；熱烈地

英文 I love you ardently.

原句 *I love thee best.*

中文 我熱切地愛著你。

039. perceive *(vt.)* 察覺，感知，理解

英文 Nothing is either good or bad unless one perceives it as such.

原句 *There is nothing either good or bad but thinking makes it so*

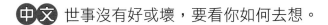

中文 世事沒有好或壞，要看你如何去想。

---

040. reflection *(n.)* 反射，反映，反省

英文 A dream itself is a reflection.

原句 *A dream itself is but a shadow.*

中文 夢本身只是個幻影。

• track *008*

---

041. distract *(vt.)* 轉移，使分心，困擾

英文 He admits that he feels distracted.

原句 *He does confess he feels himself distracted*

中文 他承認自己有點心神不寧。

---

042. relief *(n.)* 緩和，減輕，慰藉，救濟

英文 It's a relief to hear that he's taking an interest in something.

原句 *It doth much content me to hear him so inclined.*

中文 聽到他對某件事情感興趣，讓人覺得安心。

---

043. sugar over *(ph.)* 粉飾

---

044. innocent *(adj.)* 無辜的，無罪的，天真的

英文 It's a fact that we often sugar over the devil himself with an innocent face and saintly actions.

原句 *'Tis too much proved, that with devotion's visage and pious action we do sugar o'er.*

中文 事實上，我們經常用無辜的表情和聖者般的行為，來掩飾內心的惡魔。

045. question *(n.)* 問題，難題，疑問

英文 To be, or not to be: that is the question.

原句 *To be, or not to be: that is the question.*

中文 要生還是要死，這是問題所在。

046. yourselves *(pron.)* 你們自己，(加強語氣，強調) 你們親自

英文 God has given you one face and you make another for yourselves.

原句 *God has given you one face and you make yourselves another.*

中文 上帝給你們一張臉，你們自己還要另外造一張。

047. ignore *(vt.)* 不顧，不理會，忽視

048. in high places *(ph.)* 有權勢的人

英文 We can't ignore madness in high places.

原句 *Madness in great ones must not unwatch'd go.*

中文 我們不能忽視地位重要的人發瘋了。

呼應懷疑主義思想

　　法國文藝復興時期的人文主義哲學家蒙田認為《哈姆雷特》反應了當時的懷疑主義思想。在此之前，人文主義者米蘭多拉辯稱人是上帝最偉大的造物，具有上帝的形象，並可以選擇自己的本性；然而這種觀點在蒙田的《隨筆集》中被駁斥。哈姆雷特的「人類是一件多麼了不得的傑作」與蒙田的思想相呼應，但學者無法確認莎士比亞直接引用了蒙田的作品，還是倆人一同對時代做出了類似的反應。

●track *009*

---

049. meek *(adj.)* 溫順的；懦弱的

---

050. discretion *(n.)* 謹慎，考慮周到

英文 Don't be too meek either, but let your own discretion be your guide.

原句 *Be not too tame neither, but let your own discretion*

中文 不過也不要太過溫順，要用審慎的態度去判斷事情的輕重。

051. exaggeration *(n.)* 誇張，誇大，誇張語言

英文 Exaggeration has no place in the theater, where the purpose is to represent reality, holding a mirror up to nature.

原句 *For anything so overdone is from the purpose of playing, whose end, both at the first and now, was and is to hold, as 'twere, the mirror up to nature.*

中文 太誇張的表演會失去戲劇的目的，畢竟演戲的目的是要像鏡子般反映人性。

052. flatter *(vt.)* 諂媚，使高興，相片比本人好看

英文 Don't think I'm flattering you.

原句 *Do not think I flatter.*

中文 別以為我在恭維你。

053. not take one's eyes off *(ph.)* 一直注視，目不轉睛

英文 Don't take your eyes off my uncle.

原句 *Observe mine uncle.*

中文 不要讓你的視線離開我的叔父。

054. behaviour *(n.)* 行為

055. astonish *(vt.)* 使驚訝

英文 Your behaviour has amazed and astonished her.

原句 *Your behavior hath struck her into amazement and admiration.*

中文 你的行為使她非常詫異。

056. insanity *(n.)* 瘋狂，荒唐

057. out of control *(ph.)* 失去控制

英文 I don't like the way he's acting, and it's not safe for us to let his insanity get out of control.

原句 *I like him not, nor stands it safe with us to let his madness range.*

中文 我不喜歡他，而且任由他這樣瘋癲胡鬧下去，對我們也不利。

058. whirlpool *(n.)* 漩渦

059. draw *(vt.)* 畫，拉，引出，吸引

英文 When a king dies, he doesn't die alone but, like a whirlpool, draws others with him.

原句 *The cease of majesty dies not alone, but, like a gulf, doth draw what's near it with it.*

中文 國王的逝世不只是一人之死，而是像漩渦，會把其他的人事捲進去。

060. tapestry *(n.)* 掛毯，壁毯，帷幕

英文 I'll hide behind the tapestry to hear what they say.

原句 *Behind the arras I'll convey myself to hear the process.*

中文 我會躲在帷幕後面偷聽他們的談話內容。

---

061. enough *(adj.)* 足夠的，充足的；*(adv.)* 足夠地，
充足地；*(n.)* 足夠，充足

英文 Isn't there enough rain in heaven to wash it clean as snow?

原句 *Is there not rain enough in the sweet heavens to wash it white as snow?*

中文 天堂就沒有足夠的雨，把它沖洗得像雪一樣乾淨嗎？

---

062. stick *(vt.)* 刺，黏貼，伸出；*(vi.)* 黏住，伸出；
(n.) 枝條，棒狀物

---

063. struggle *(vi.)*, *(n.)* 奮鬥，努力，掙扎

英文 My soul is stuck to sin, and the more it struggles to break free, the more it sticks.

原句 *O limèd soul that, struggling to be free art more engaged!*

中文 我的靈魂像被黏住，越是掙紮黏得越緊。

---

064. villain *(n.)* 惡棍，壞人，罪犯

英文 A villain kills my father, and I, my father's only son, send this same villain to heaven.

原句 *A villain kills my father; and for that, I, his sole son, do this same villain send to heaven*

中文 一個惡棍殺害我父親，我是我父親的獨子，因而也殺了惡棍。

065. rudely *(adv.)* 無禮地，粗暴地

英文 What have I done that you dare to talk to me so rudely?

原句 *What have I done, that thou darest wag thy tongue in noise so rude against me?*

中文 我做了什麼事，你膽敢對我說話這麼無禮？

066. look *(vt.)* 留心，期待；*(vi.)* 看，留神，看起來；*(n.)* 看，臉色，外表

英文 You're making me look into my very soul.

原句 *Thou turn'st mine eyes into my very soul.*

中文 你使我看進我的靈魂深處。

067. dagger *(vt.)* 用短劍刺；*(n.)* 短劍，匕首

068. stab *(vt.)*, *(vi.)* 刺，戳，刺傷

英文 Your words are like daggers stabbing my ears.

原句 *These words like daggers enter in my ears.*

中文 你的話像刀子一樣刺入我的耳朵。

069. sharpen *(vt.)* 削尖，使敏銳，加劇；*(vi.)* 變鋒利，變得敏銳

英文 I've come to sharpen your somewhat dull appetite for revenge.

原句 *This visitation is but to whet thy almost blunted purpose.*

中文 我是來讓你稍嫌遲鈍的復仇之心，變得敏銳一些。

---

070. fake *(vt.)*, *(vi.)* 偽造，假裝；*(adj.)* 假的，冒充的；*(n.)* 冒牌貨，騙子

英文 My madness is fake.

原句 *I essentially am not in madness.*

中文 我是裝瘋的。

第四幕
第一景

● track *012*

---

071. privately *(adv.)* 私下地，不公開地

英文 Let us speak privately awhile, please.

原句 *Bestow this place on us a little while.*

中文 請讓我們單獨說一下話。

---

072. threat *(n.)* 威脅，恐嚇，構成威脅的人 (或事物)

英文 His wildness is a threat to all of us.

原句 *His liberty is full of threats to all*

中文 他的瘋狂會對大家造成威脅。

---

073. corpse *(n.)* 屍體，殘骸

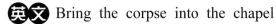 Bring the corpse into the chapel

(原句) *Bring the body into the chapel*

(中文) 把屍體送到禮拜堂。

第四幕
第一景

● track *013*

---

074. advice *(n.)* 勸告，忠告，消息

---

075. rather than *(ph.)* 而不是……

(英文) Don't believe that I'd take your advice rather than keep my own secret.

(原句) *(Don't believe) That I can keep your counsel and not mine own.*

(中文) 不要相信我會聽從你的勸告，而把我的祕密告訴你。

---

076. squeeze *(vt.)* 榨，擠，緊抱；*(vi.)* 榨，擠，壓榨；*(n.)* 緊抱，壓榨

---

077. sponge *(vt.)* , *(vi.)* (用海綿) 吸取，似海綿般地吸收；*(n.)* 海綿

(英文) When he needs what you have found out, he can just squeeze you like a sponge and you'll be dry again.

原句 *When he needs what you have gleaned, it is but squeezing you and, sponge, you shall be dry again.*

中文 當他需要知道你搜集了些什麼消息，只要把你當作是海綿擠一下，擠完不久你就又乾了。

●track *014*

---

078. apply...to *(ph.)* 適用於，向……申請 (或要求)

英文 But we mustn't apply strict law to him.

原句 *Yet must not we put the strong law on him.*

中文 不過我們不能對他施以嚴刑峻法。

---

079. require *(vt.)* 需要

英文 A terminal disease requires extreme treatment.

原句 *Diseases desperate grown by desperate appliance are relieved*

中文 嚴重的病症需要猛藥才能治療。

---

080. skinny *(adj.)* 似皮的，極瘦的，吝嗇的

---

081. meal *(vi.)* 進餐；*(n.)* 進餐，膳食

英文 A fat king and a skinny beggar are just two dishes at the same meal.

原句 *Your fat king and your lean beggar is but variable service—two dishes, but to one table.*

中文 胖國王和瘦乞丐不過是兩盤菜色不同的菜,但被放在同一個餐桌上。

---

082. favorable *(adj.)* 贊同的,有利的,討人喜歡的

英文 The ship is set to sail and the wind is favorable.

原句 *The bark is ready and the wind at help.*

中文 船已經準備妥當,而且又順風。

---

083. waste *(vt.)* 浪費,消耗,使荒蕪;*(vi.)* 被浪費,消瘦;*(adj.)* 廢棄的;*(n.)* 浪費,廢料,荒地

英文 Don't waste any time.

原句 *Delay it not.*

中文 不要耽誤時間。

第四幕
第四景

●track *015*

---

084. invade *(vt.)* , *(vi.)* 侵入,侵略,侵犯

英文 They're on their way to invade some part of Poland.

原句 *Against some part of Poland*

中文 他們要去攻打波蘭的某處。

---

085. tell the truth *(ph.)* 講實話

---

086. patch *(vt.)* 修補，拼湊；*(n.)* 補釘，貼片，小塊土

英文 To tell the truth, we're fighting to win a little patch of ground that's not worth anything.

原句 *Truly to speak, and with no addition, we go to gain a little patch of ground that hath in it no profit but the name.*

中文 老實說，我們只是要去佔領一塊沒有利益可言的小土地。

---

087. defend *(vt.)* 防禦，保護，為……辯護；(vi) 防禦，保護

英文 So then the Polack won't be willing to defend it.

原句 *Why, then the Polack never will defend it.*

中文 那麼，波蘭人不防禦這塊土地了。

---

088. motivation *(n.)* 動機，刺激，推動

---

089. means *(n.)* 手段，方法，工具

英文 I have the motivation, the willpower, the ability, and the means to do it.

原句 *I have cause and will and strength and means to do 't.*

中文 我有動機、信念、能力和手段去做這件事。

華麗複雜的語言特色

　　莎士比亞的作品給人第一印象就是語言複雜、華麗、難懂。然而，它依然能勝任劇院的演出任務。例如《哈姆雷特》中的語言大多是宮廷用語：優雅、詼諧。事實上，哈姆雷特這個角色的語言修辭超群，他在許多特定場合下會使用簡潔直接的語言，譬如表述自己對母親的內在感情時，他說：「它們不過是悲哀的裝飾和衣服；可是我鬱結的心事卻是無法表現出來的。」巧妙地透過雙關語表達想法，但又不那麼容易看穿。

●track *016*

090. insistent *(adj.)* 堅持的，持續的，顯著的

英文 She's insistent.

原句 *She is importunate.*

中文 她堅持。

091. talk about …a lot *(ph.)* 說了很多關於……的事

英文 She talks about her father a lot.

原句 *She speaks much of her father.*

中文 她說了很多她父親的事。

---

092. conspiracy *(n.)* 陰謀，謀叛，共謀

英文 She hears there are conspiracies around the world.

原句 *she hears there's tricks i' th' world.*

中文 她聽說這世界上有許多陰謀。

---

093. tell the difference between...and... *(ph.)* 分辨……和……的不同

英文 How can you tell the difference between your true lover and some other?

原句 *How should I your true love know from another one?*

中文 你要如何分辨真愛和不是真愛的不同？

---

094. keep an eye on... *(ph.)* 仔細看守，細心照顧

英文 Keep an eye on her.

原句 *Give her good watch.*

中文 好好看著她。

---

095. attack *(vt.)* , *(vi.)* 進攻，襲擊；*(n.)* 攻擊，抨擊，(疾病) 發作

---

096. battalion *(n.)* 大隊，軍隊

英文 When sorrows attack us, they don't do it with single soldiers, but in battalions.

原句 *When sorrows come, they come not single spies, but in battalions.*

中文 當悲傷來襲擊的時候，它不會單獨來，而是成群結隊前來。

---

097. end up *(ph.)* 結果成為，最終成為，以……終結

英文 How did he end up dead?

原句 *How came he dead?*

中文 他是怎麼死的？

---

098. persuasive *(adj.)* 勸說的，有說服力的

英文 If you were sane and could urge me to take revenge, you couldn't be more persuasive than you are now.

原句 *Hadst thou thy wits, and didst persuade revenge, it could not move thus.*

中文 就算妳沒有瘋而且力勸我報仇，都沒有辦法比妳現在這個樣子更具有說服力。

---

099. rosemary *(n.)* 迷迭香

英文 There's rosemary, that's for remembering. Please remember me, my love.

原句 *There's rosemary, that's for remembrance; pray, love, remember.*

中文 迷迭香代表回憶，我的愛，請記得我。

第四幕
第六景

100. speechless *(adj.)* 說不出話來的，不能用言語表達的

英文 I've got things to tell you that will make you speechless.

原句 *I have words to speak in thine ear will make thee dumb.*

中文 我有話要告訴你，你聽了之後會說不出話來。

101. deliver *(vt.)* 投遞，運送，發表，生小孩；*(vi.)* 投遞，送貨

英文 I'll show you where to deliver these letters.

原句 *I will give you way for these your letters.*

中文 我會指引你們要去哪裏送信。

第四幕
第七景

102. immediate *(adj.)* 立即的，目前的

英文 But tell me why you didn't take immediate action against his criminal acts.

原句 *But tell me why you proceeded not against these feats.*

中文 告訴我你為何不馬上採取行動，懲戒這樣的犯罪行為。

103. handwriting *(n.)* 書寫，手寫，筆跡

英文 Do you recognize the handwriting?

原句 *Know you the hand?*

中文 你認得這個筆跡嗎？

104. clue *(vt.)* 為……提供線索；*(n.)* 提示，線索，跡象

英文 I have no clue.

原句 *I'm lost in it.*

中文 我一無所知。

105. blame *(vt.)* 責備，指責，把……歸咎於；*(n.)* 責備，指責

英文 When he dies, no one will be blamed.

原句 *For his death no wind of blame shall breathe.*

中文 他一旦死了，沒有人會被怪罪的。

106. excess *(adj.)* 過量的，額外的；*(n.)* 超過，過量，無節制

英文 Even a good thing can grow too big and die from its own excess.

原句 *For goodness, growing to a pleurisy, dies in his own too-much.*

中文 好的事情變得過度時，就會因為太超過而由盈轉虧。

107. prepare *(vt.)* 準備，做飯菜；*(vi.)* 準備，預備

108. prove *(vt.)* 證明，證實，顯示；*(vi.)* 證明是；
原來是

英文 What would you be prepared to do to prove you are your father's son, in action rather than words?'

原句 *What would you undertake to show yourself in deed your father's son more than in words?*

中文 你打算如何用行動來證明你是你父親的兒子，而不是只有說說而已？

109. dab *(vt.)*, *(vi.)* 輕拍，輕觸，輕塗；*(n.)* 輕拍，
輕塗，小塊，一點點

英文 I'll put a little dab of something on my sword.

原句 *I'll anoint my sword.*

中文 我會在我的劍上塗點東西。

110. calm down *(ph.)* 平靜下來

英文 I worked so hard to calm him down.

原句 *How much I had to do to calm his rage!*

中文 我很努力要讓他平靜下來。

---

111. parchment *(n.)* 羊皮紙；仿羊皮紙

英文 Isn't the parchment of a legal document made of sheepskin?

原句 *Is not parchment made of sheepskins?*

中文 契約不都是羊皮紙做的嗎？

---

112. recover *(vt.)* 恢復，重新獲得；*(vi.)* 恢復，恢復健康

英文 He'll recover his sanity there.

原句 *He shall recover his wits there.*

中文 他會在那把瘋病養好。

---

113. rot *(vt.)* 使腐爛，使腐敗；*(vi.)*, *(n.)* 腐爛，腐敗

英文 How long will a man lie in his grave before his body starts to rot?

原句 *How long will a man lie i' the earth ere he rot?*

中文 一個人躺在墳墓裡多久，他的身體才會開始腐爛？

---

114. carry *(vt.)* 背，提，運送，傳達；*(vi.)* 被攜帶，被搬運

英文 He carried me on his back a thousand times.

原句 *He hath borne me on his back a thousand times.*

中文 他把我揹在背上有上千次。

---

115. bury *(vt.)* 埋葬，掩藏，使沉浸

英文 Do you think Alexander the Great looked like this when he was buried?

原句 *Dost thou think Alexander looked o' this fashion i' th' earth?*

中文 你想亞歷山大大帝被埋葬後，也會是這個樣子嗎？

---

116. bloom *(vi.)* 開花，繁榮；*(n.)* 開花，最佳時期

---

117. flesh *(n.)* 肉體；肉慾

英文 Lay her in the ground, and let violets bloom from her lovely and pure flesh!

原句 *Lay her i' th' earth and from her fair and unpolluted flesh may violets spring!*

中文 把她放到土裏吧！她美麗純潔的身軀會長出紫羅蘭。

---

118. hold off *(ph.)* 保持距離，使不接近

英文 Hold off burying her until I've caught her in my arms once more.

原句 *Hold off the earth awhile till I have caught her once more in mine arms.*

中文 先別埋葬她，讓我再抱抱她。

---

119. add...together *(ph.)* 將……相加

英文 I loved Ophelia. Forty thousand brothers, if you added all their love together, couldn't match mine.

原句 *I loved ophelia. Forty thousand brothers could not with all their quantity of love make up my sum.*

中文 我愛奧菲麗雅，四萬兄弟的愛加起來，也抵不過我對她的愛。

第五幕
第二景

● track *020*

---

120. count *(vt.)* 計算，將……計算在內，認為；*(vi.)* 計數，有重要意義；*(n.)* 計數

英文 A human life is hardly long enough to count to one in.

原句 *A man's life's no more than to say "one."*

中文 人生苦短，還沒數到一就結束了。

---

121. gaze *(vi.)*, *(n.)* 凝視，注視

英文 He can find an equal only when he gazes into a mirror.

原句 *His semblable is his mirror.*

中文 在鏡子裡看到的他，是唯一可以和他相提並論的對手。

---

122. be supposed to *(ph.)* 期望，認為必須，認為應該

英文 If something is supposed to happen now, it will. If it's supposed to happen later, it won't happen now.

原句 *If it be not to come, it will be now. If it be not now, yet it will come.*

中文 命中註定是現在，就不會發生在未來；假如註定不會是現在，就會發生在未來。

---

123. make fun of *(ph.)* 嘲弄

英文 You're making fun of me.

原句 *You mock me*

中文 你取笑我。

---

124. goblet *(n.)* 高腳杯，無柄酒杯

英文 Put the goblets of wine on that table.

原句 *Set me the stoups of wine upon that table.*

中文 在桌上擺好酒杯。

---

125. ancient *(adj.)* 古代的，古老的；*(n.)* 老人，古代人

英文 I'm more like an ancient Roman than a Dane.

原句 *I am more an antique Roman than a Dane.*

中文 我雖然是丹麥人，卻更像古羅馬人。

劇情簡介
《李爾王》
(King Lear)

　　英格蘭的國王李爾王 (King Lear) 已經八十幾歲了，他有感於自己年事已高，無法再像從前一樣順遂地處理朝政，便決定將政權交給三個女兒。他將國土劃分為三部份，在分封國土時，告訴女兒們，只要她們當眾說出誰最愛他、最有孝心，他就會賜予最大的恩惠。

　　大女兒及二女兒巧言令色地哄騙了老國王，老國王很高興地把國土分封給她們，輪到三女兒寇蒂莉亞 (Cordelia) 時，由於她認為愛不應該只在於言語的表達，重要的是要有愛心，因而不願誇大其詞地說出她對父親的愛，使得她在李爾王的暴怒中被逐出王國。最後，三女兒傷心地和新婚夫婿法蘭西親王離開心愛的父親，連在一旁勸阻的忠臣肯特 (Kent) 也因李爾王的遷怒而遭到放逐。李爾王分封完所有國土之後，下令只留下一百個親衛兵隨伺，並準備輪流跟大女兒和二女兒住，然而兩個女兒得到一切之後很快就現出原形，聯手將老父趕出曾經屬

於他的王國。李爾王在憤怒、羞愧等複雜情緒的刺激之下，終於發瘋了！

另一方面，李爾王的老臣葛羅斯特 (Gloster) 遭私生子愛德蒙 (Edmund) 挑撥，誤信親生兒子愛德佳圖謀他的財產並想要謀殺他，於是四處追捕愛德佳，逃亡的愛德佳 (Edgar) 只好裝瘋避難、四處乞討。這時，離開自己王國的李爾王流落到荒郊，更遭受到暴風雨的侵襲，身邊只有弄人、忠臣肯特以及已然失明的葛羅斯特，他因誤信私生子愛德蒙，終招致了被愛德蒙與李爾王兩個女兒挖去雙眼的噩運；其實裝瘋的愛德佳也以瘋子的身分陪侍在葛羅斯特身邊，但卻不敢與父親相認，而他們一行人就一起過著四處被追殺的日子。

葛羅斯特失去雙眼後十分懊悔，並恍然明白一向信任且疼愛的私生子才是真正的背叛者，他盲目昏聵地錯怪了親生的兒子，這樣的醒悟使他想結束自己的人生，於是帶著堅定的決心執意要求死。陪伴在旁的愛德佳內心非常著急，但又不能跟父親相認，便假意帶他走上懸崖，其實只是小土台，葛羅斯特自土台跳下，雖獲重生，卻又因無法承受與親生兒子相認的激動，在悲喜交加中死去。

李爾王的三女兒聽聞老父遭到姐姐的欺凌，便與夫婿領軍攻打姐姐，試圖要幫父親討回公道，恢復父王的江山，經過一番激烈的戰鬥，三女兒兵敗被囚，李爾王眼睜睜地看著心愛的三女兒被處死，另外兩位女兒則因

互相爭鬥兩敗俱傷，愛德蒙也在與愛德佳決鬥時中劍身亡，李爾王才在此時了悟親情與愛，但一切已因他的剛愎自用而毀滅，李爾王只能為三女兒的逝去憂傷而終。

●track *021*

---

126. prefer...to (*ph.*) 寧願選擇……而不是……，更喜歡

英文 I thought the king preferred the Duke of Albany to the Duke of Cornwall.

原句 *I thought the king had more affected the Duke of Albany than Cornwall.*

中文 我認為國王喜歡奧本尼公爵比康華爾公爵更多一些。

---

127. used to (*ph.*) 過去時常，過去曾 (而現在不再) 做

英文 We used to think so too.

原句 *It did always seem so to us.*

中文 我們一向都如此認為。

---

128. look forward to (*ph.*) 期待

英文 I look forward to getting to know you better.

原句 *I must love you and sue to know you better.*

中文 我期待更認識你。

---

129. divide...into *(ph.)* 把……分成

英文 I've divided my kingdom into three parts.

原句 *know that we have divided in three our kingdom.*

中文 我已經把我的國土劃分成三部。

---

130. more than *(ph.)* 比……更多，超過

英文 I love you more than words can say.

原句 *I do love you more than words can wield the matter*

中文 我對你的愛，不是言語所能表達的。

---

131. description *(n.)* 描寫，敘述

英文 Her description falls a little short of the truth.

原句 *Only she comes too short.*

中文 她的描述不能完全說明事實。

---

132. be poor in *(ph.)* 貧乏的，不充足的

英文 But I'm not poor in love—my love is bigger than my words are.

原句 *And yet not so, since I am sure my love's more ponderous than my tongue.*

中文 我的愛並不貧乏，我的愛比我的言語要更豐富。

---

133. try again *(ph.)* 再試一次

英文 Nothing will get you nothing. Try again.

原句 *Nothing will come of nothing. Speak again.*

中文 什麼都不說 (本句的**nothing**指什麼都不說) 會讓你得不到任何東西。妳再說說看！

134. revise *(vt.)* 修訂，校訂，修改；*(vi.)* , *(n.)* 修訂，校訂

英文 Revise your statement, or you may damage your inheritance.

原句 *Mend your speech a little lest it mar your fortunes.*

中文 修正你說的話，否則你會得不到遺產。

135. honor *(vt.)* 使增光，給……以榮譽；*(n.)* 榮譽，信譽，光榮的事或人

英文 I've always honored you as my king.

原句 *I have ever honored as my king.*

中文 我向來敬你為我的君王。

136. instead of *(ph.)* 代替，寧願

英文 If I decide to do something, then I do it instead of talking about it.

原句 *Since what I well intend, I'll do't before I speak.*

中文 假如我要做某件事凡，就會去做而不會在嘴巴上說。

137. irrelevant *(ph.)* 沒有關係的，不恰當的

英文 Love's not love when it gets mixed up with irrelevant outside matters.

原句 *Love's not love when it is mingled with regards that stands aloof from th' entire point.*

中文 愛情裡面要是攙雜了和它本身無關的算計，那就不是真的愛情。

---

138. deceitful *(adj.)* 騙人的，欺詐的，虛假的

---

139. have something up one's sleeve *(ph.)* 計謀，錦囊妙計，應急計劃

英文 Time will tell what you've got up your sleeve. You can be deceitful in the short term, but eventually truth will come out.

原句 *Time shall unfold what plighted cunning hides, who covers faults at last with shame derides.*

中文 時間會揭穿你們的陰謀，你們只能騙得過一時，最後真相一定會大白。

真實反映封建衰亡

《李爾王》真實地反映了資本主義世界中，資本原始積累時期動盪不安的英國社會面貌，也是作者對專制王權的批判和對人性的歌頌。受狡詐冷酷女兒和陰險殘暴女婿的虐待，李爾王由專橫暴虐、剛愎自用的統治者，一下子變成了流浪的乞丐般的國王，這個過程具體反映文藝復興晚期封建階級走向衰亡的歷史；展現封建主義解體、資本主義興起，人與人之間赤裸裸的金錢關係，替代舊的綱紀倫常的歷史真實。

●track *022*

| **140.** | finish *(vt.)* 結束，完成，潤飾；*(vi.)* 結束，
完成工作；*(n.)* 結束，拋光，末道漆 |

英文 It's a letter from my brother that I haven't finished reading yet.

原句 *It is a letter from my brother that I have not all o'er-read.*

中文 這是我哥哥寫給我的信，我還沒有看完。

| **141.** | proceed *(vi.)* 繼續進行，著手 |

英文 I know exactly how to proceed.

原句 *I see the business.*

中文 我確實知道該如何進行。

●track *023*

| **142.** | scold *(vt.)* , *(vi.)* , *(n.)* 責罵 |

英文 Did my father hit one of my attendants for scolding his fool?

原句 *Did my father strike my gentleman for chiding of his fool?*

中文 我的父親因為我的侍衛罵他的弄臣，所以動手打他嗎？

---

143. wield *(vt.)* 揮舞 (劍)，行使 (權力)

英文 That useless old man still thinks he can wield all the powers he's given away.

原句 *Idle old man that still would manage those authorities that he hath given away!*

中文 這老廢物還認為他可以行使他已經放棄的權力。

第一幕
第四景

● track *024*

---

144. remind *(vt.)* 提醒，使想起

英文 You're just reminding me of something I've also noticed.

原句 *Thou but rememberest me of mine own conception.*

中文 你正提醒我一件我已經注意到的事。

---

145. put an end to *(ph.)* 結束，廢止

英文 I thought you could put an end to all this if I told you about it.

原句 *I had thought by making this well known unto you to have found a safe redress.*

中文 我本來以為告訴你情況，你就會讓事情告一段落。

---

146. grip *(vt.)* 握 (或咬，夾) 牢，控制，掌握； *(vi.)* 握 (或咬，夾) 牢； *(n.)* 理解，緊握，掌握

---

147. screwy *(adj.)* 古怪的，怪誕的

英文 Either his mind is losing its grip or his judgment is screwy.

原句 *Either his notion weakens, or his discernings are lethargied.*

中文 他的智力衰退了，還是他無法清楚判斷事情。

---

148. meticulously *(adv.)* 極注意地，一絲不苟地

英文 My knights are the finest men who can attend a king, and they meticulously uphold their reputation.

原句 *My train are men of choice and rarest parts that all particulars of duty know and in the most exact regard support.*

中文 我的侍衛都是最有品行的人，他們的一舉一動，都無愧於騎士之名。

第一幕
第五景

●track *025*

---

149. treat *(vt.)* 對待，把……看作，款待； *(vi.)* , *(n.)* 請客

英文 Your other daughter will treat you kindly, you'll see.

原句 *Shalt see thy other daughter will use thee kindly.*

中文 你終將會知道你的另外一個女兒會善待你。

---

150. **go mad** *(ph.)* 發瘋，失去理智

英文 Keep me balanced and sane. I don't want to go mad.

原句 *Keep me in temper. I would not be mad.*

中文 讓我保持鎮定清醒，我不想發瘋。

● track *026*

---

151. **leak out** *(ph.)* 洩露情報

英文 It has leaked out that you're hiding here.

原句 *Intelligence is given where you are hid.*

中文 你藏身在這裏的消息已經被走漏出去了。

---

152. **pretend** *(vt.)* , *(vi.)* 假裝；*(adj.)* 假裝的

英文 I have to pretend to threaten you with my sword.

原句 *In cunning I must draw my sword upon you.*

中文 我必須假裝拔劍刺你。

---

153. **mumble** *(vt.)* , *(vi.)* 含糊地說；*(n.)* 含糊的話

154. appeal to *(ph.)* 向⋯⋯呼籲，懇求，訴諸

英文 He was mumbling some black magic spells, appealing to the moon to help him in his evil plans.

原句 *(Here stood he in the dark, his sharp sword out,) mumbling of wicked charms, conjuring the moon To stand auspicious mistress.*

中文 (他站在黑暗中，拔出他鋒利的劍)，口中喃喃念著咒語，行妖法請月亮協助他完成邪惡的計畫。

155. no surprise *(ph.)* 不讓人意外

英文 Then it's no surprise they had a bad influence on him.

原句 *No marvel then, though he were ill affected.*

中文 他會被他們帶壞，一點都不讓人意外。

第二幕第二景

• track *027*

156. have nothing to do with *(ph.)* 避開，與⋯⋯無關

英文 I've got nothing to do with you.

原句 *I have nothing to do with thee*

中文 我不想和你扯上關係。

157. scoundrel *(n.)* 壞蛋，惡棍

英文 Don't run away, scoundrel.

原句 *Stand, rogue.*

中文 別跑，你這流氓。

---

158. messenger *(n.)* 送信人，使者，傳令員

英文 The messengers from our sister and the king.

原句 *What's the matter here?*

中文 這使者一個是我姐姐派來的，一個是國王派來的。

兩個主線強化主題

　　《李爾王》中有兩個主線，一條圍繞著李爾王及三個女兒；一條線索圍繞葛羅斯特伯爵及兩個兒子。李爾和葛羅斯特都是先昏後明，先惡後善，先富後貧，先福後苦；而李爾的三個女兒和葛羅斯特的兩個兒子都真假有別，善惡顯見，或前後不一，或始終如一。當李爾王不過是李爾的時候，當伯爵不過是淒慘難民的時候，他們才恢複了人的本來面目，恢復了人的良知，也只有在這樣的時候才能看出周圍人的本來面目，看出人們的原形。

159. quarrel *(vi.)* , *(n.)* 爭吵，不和

英文 What did you start quarreling over?

原句 *How fell you out?*

中文 你們為什麼爭吵？

160. offend *(vt.)* 冒犯，傷害……的感情，使不開心；
(vi.) 違反，引起不悅

英文 How did you offend him?

原句 *What was th' offense you gave him?*

中文 你是怎樣冒犯他的？

第二幕
第三景

● track *028*

161. declare *(vt.)* 宣告，聲明，申報；*(vi.)* 聲明，表示

162. outlaw *(vt.)* 將……放逐；*(n.)* 罪犯，被放逐者

英文 I heard myself declared an outlaw and escaped capture
by hiding in the trunk of a hollow tree.

原句 *I heard myself proclaimed and by the happy hollow
of a tree escaped the hunt.*

中文 聽說他們已經通緝我，幸虧我躲進一株空心的樹幹裡，
沒有被逮到。

● track 029

---

163. according to (*ph.*) 根據，按照

英文 According to what I heard, they had no travel plans as of last night.

原句 *As I learn'd, the night before there was no purpose in them of this remove*

中文 據我所知，他們到昨晚還沒有離開的計畫。

---

164. agonizing (*ph.*) 令人苦悶的，令人痛苦難忍的

英文 The agonizing feeling makes my heart hurt.

原句 *O, how this mother swells up toward my heart!*

中文 我覺得一陣酸楚湧上心頭。

---

165. inform (*vt.*) 通知，報告；(*vi.*) 告發，告密

英文 I informed them as much.

原句 *I have informed them so.*

中文 我已經和他們說過了。

---

166. out of order (*ph.*) 發生故障

---

167. properly (*adv.*) 恰當地，正確地，有禮貌地

英文 When our bodies are out of order, our minds can't

function properly.

原句 *We are not ourselves when nature, being oppressed, commands the mind to suffer with the body.*

中文 當我們身體不舒服時，內心也會跟著抑鬱不安。

---

168. neglect *(vt.)*, *(n.)* 忽略，疏忽，疏漏

---

169. obligation *(n.)* (道義上或法律上的) 義務，責任

英文 I can't believe my sister would neglect her obligations in any way.

原句 *I cannot think my sister in the least would fail her obligation.*

中文 我不相信我的姐姐會對她份內的事有所疏忽。

---

170. splinter *(vt.)* 使裂成碎片；*(vi.)* 裂成碎片；*(n.)* 碎片

英文 I have a good reason to cry, but my heart will splinter into a hundred thousand pieces before I let myself cry.

原句 *I have full cause of weeping, but this heart shall break into a hundred thousand flaws or ere I'll weep.*

中文 我雖然有充分的理由哭泣，可是我寧願讓這顆心碎成萬片，也不願流下一滴淚來。

反映失地農民的苦難

　　《李爾王》真實地反映了當時廣大人民的苦難。李爾王流落荒郊，飽嚐暴風雨襲擊的苦楚，隨著地位的改變，他不由聯想起成千上萬無家可歸的窮人。他激動地說：「衣不蔽體的不幸的人們，無論你們在什麼地方，都得忍受這樣無情暴風雨的襲擊，你們的頭上沒有片瓦遮身，你們的腹中饑腸雷動，你們的衣服千瘡百孔，怎麼抵擋得了這樣的氣候呢？」這段話真實地揭示了圈地運動中失地農民流落異鄉、饑寒交迫的慘狀。

第二幕
第一景

●track *030*

171. aside from *(ph.)* 除此之外

英文 Who's there, aside from this foul weather?

原句 *Who's there, besides foul weather?*

中文 除了惡劣的天氣，還有誰在這兒？

172. soothe *(vt.)* 安慰，緩和，減輕；*(vi.)* 起撫慰 (或鎮定) 作用

173. wound *(vt.)* 使受傷；*(vi.)* 傷害；*(n.)* 創傷，傷口，傷害

英文 Nobody was with him but the fool, who's trying to soothe the wounds in the king's heart with jokes.

原句 *None but the fool, who labors to outjest his heartfelt injuries.*

中文 只有弄臣跟著他，努力說笑話替他排解內心的傷痛。

174. assign *(vt.)* 分配，分派，指定

175. job *(n.)* 工作，費力的事情，職責，成果

英文 I'm a nobleman, and I know what I'm doing in assigning this job to you.

原句 *I am a gentleman of blood and breeding, and from some knowledge and assurance offer this office to you.*

中文 我是一個有身份的人，而且我相信你，所以把這件事交待給你。

●track 031

176. terrify *(vt.)* 使害怕，使恐怖

177. prowl *(vt.)* 潛行，暗中巡行；*(vi.)* (野獸等) 四處覓食，潛行；*(n.)* 四處覓食，搜尋

英文 The angry skies terrify the animals that usually prowl in the dark, making them stay in their caves.

原句 *The wrathful skies gallow the very wanderers of the dark and make them keep their caves.*

中文 惡劣的天候讓經常潛行於黑暗中的野獸，嚇得躲進洞裡不敢出來。

178. bring to light *(ph.)* 揭露

179. enemy *(n.)* 敵人，敵軍；*(adj.)* 敵人的，敵方的

英文 Let the gods who stirred up this dreadful storm bring their enemies to light.

原句 *Let the great gods that keep this dreadful pudder o'er our heads find out their enemies now.*

中文 讓那些在我們頭頂掀起這可怕風暴的眾神，找到他們的敵人吧。

180. prophecy *(n.)* 預言，預言能力

英文 This is the prophecy that the wizard Merlin will make one day. I'm a little ahead of my time in saying it now.

原句 *This prophecy Merlin shall make, for I live before his time.*

中文 巫師梅林之後將會作出這番預言，但因為我在他之前出生，所以才能夠現在先說出來。

第三幕
第二景

●track *032*

181. uncivilized *(adj.)* 野蠻的，未開化的

英文 That's uncivilized and unnatural!

原句 *Most savage and unnatural!*

中文 這太野蠻、太不近人情！

182. feud *(n.)* 世仇，仇恨，爭吵 *(vi.)* 世代結仇，爭吵

英文：There's a feud between the two dukes.

原句 *There's a division betwixt the dukes.*

中文 兩個公爵現在已經有了裂痕。

第三幕
第四景

● track *033*

---

183. entrance *(n.)* 入口，登場，入學

英文 My lord, here is the entrance.

原句 *Good my lord, enter here.*

中文 陛下，請從這裏進入。

---

184. disappear *(vi.)* 消失，突然離開，滅絕

英文 But whenever you feel a larger pain, the smaller one disappears.

原句 *But where the greater malady is fixed, the lesser is scarce felt.*

中文 但當一個人身染重病時，就不會感覺到比較小的痛楚。

---

185. protect…from *(ph.)* 保護某人或某物免於……，防衛

英文 This storm protects me from thoughts that would hurt me more.

原句 *This tempest will not give me leave to ponder on things would hurt me more.*

中文 暴風雨讓我不再去想那些使我傷心的事情。

---

186. compose oneself *(ph.)* 鎮定

英文 Please compose youself, uncle.

原句 *Prithee, nuncle, be contented.*

中文 老伯伯,請你冷靜一點。

---

187. harsh *(adj.)* 粗糙的,刺耳的,嚴厲的

英文 I couldn't bear to obey all of your daughters' harsh orders.

原句 *My duty cannot suffer to obey in all your daughters' hard commands.*

中文 我無法服從你的女兒們給我的嚴苛命令。

---

188. in private *(ph.)* 私下地

英文 Let me ask you something in private.

原句 *Let me ask you one word in private.*

中文 讓我私下問你話。

---

189. blame *(vt.)* 責備,指責,歸因於; *(n.)* 責備,指責

英文 Can you blame him?

原句 *Canst thou blame him?*

中文 你能怪他嗎?

---

190. disown *(vt.)* 否認,聲明和……斷絕關係

英文 I had a son, whom I've legally disowned.

原句 *I had a son, now outlawed from my blood.*

中文 我有一個兒子,我現在已經跟他斷絕關係了。

---

191. not just because...but because *(ph.)*
不只是由於……還因為

英文 Now I realize your brother tried to kill your father not just because your brother is an evil man, but because your father deserved it by being wicked himself.

原句 *I now perceive it was not altogether your brother's evil disposition made him seek his death, but a provoking merit set a-work by a reprovable badness in himself.*

中文 我現在才知道你哥哥想要謀害你的父親，並不完全出於惡毒的本性，多半是你父親也有錯，才會引發他的動機。

---

192. deal with *(ph.)* 與……相關，對待，處理

英文 If this letter is right, you've got a lot to deal with.

原句 *If the matter of this paper be certain, you have mighty business in hand.*

中文 假如信上所說的事情屬實，那你就有很多事要去處理。

---

193. **do what one can** *(ph.)* 盡⋯⋯人的能力

英文 I'll do what I can to make you even more comfortable.

原句 *I will piece out the comfort with what addition I can.*

中文 我會盡我的能力讓你們再舒適一些。

---

194. **in a daze** *(ph.)* 處於茫然的狀態

英文 Please don't stand there in a daze.

原句 *Stand you not so amazed.*

中文 不要這樣呆呆地站著。

---

195. **ruin** *(vt.)* 使毀滅，使成廢墟；*(vi.)* 毀滅，
變成廢墟；*(n.)* 毀滅，廢墟，遺跡

---

196. **disguise** *(vt.)* , *(n.)* 假扮，偽裝，掩飾

英文 I feel so sorry for him that my tears are starting to ruin my disguise.

原句 *My tears begin to take his part so much. They'll mar my counterfeiting.*

中文 我為他感到難過，流下來的眼淚開始破壞我的偽裝。

---

197. **lie down** *(ph.)* 平臥，稍做休息

英文 Please lie down and rest a while, my lord.

原句 *Now, good my lord, lie here and rest awhile.*

中文 陛下，您還是躺下來休息一會。

---

198. overheard (overhear 的過去式) *(vt.)* , *(vi.)*
無意中聽到，偷聽到

英文 I've overheard people plotting to kill him.

原句 *I have o'erheard a plot of death upon him.*

中文 我無意中聽到有人要謀殺他。

● track *036*

---

199. land *(vt.)* 使登陸，使降落，卸貨；*(vi.)*
登陸，降落；*(n.)* 陸地，土地

英文 The French army has landed

原句 *The army of France is landed.*

中文 法蘭西軍隊已經上岸了。

---

200. immediately *(adv.)* 立即地，直接地

英文 Tell the Duke of Albany to prepare for war immediately.

原句 *Advise the duke where you are going, to a most festinate preparation.*

中文 你去告訴奧本尼公爵立刻準備迎戰。

201. condemn *(vt.)* 責難，譴責，宣告……有罪

202. trial *(n.)* 試用，考驗，審判

英文 I can't condemn him to death without a formal trial, but I'm powerful enough that I can still do something to express my anger.

原句 *Though well we may not pass upon his life without the form of justice, yet our power shall do a courtesy to our wrath.*

中文 雖然在沒有經過正式的審判前，我們不能就把他判處死刑，可是我握有的權力還是可以讓我們的洩憤。

203. connection *(n.)* 連接，聯絡，關係

英文 And what's your connection with the traitors who landed in our kingdom recently?

原句 *And what confederacy have you with the traitors late footed in the kingdom?*

中文 你跟那些最近進入國境的叛徒們有什麼關係？

204. punish *(vt.)* 懲罰，處罰

英文 But soon I'll see the gods punish you for your lack of respect to your father.

原句 *But I shall see The wingèd vengeance overtake such children.*

中文 不過我很快就會看到你，因為沒有善待自己的父親而遭天譴。

205. lunatic *(n.)* 瘋子；*(adj.)* 瘋的，愚妄的

英文 As a wandering lunatic, he can go anywhere he wants.

原句 *His roguish madness allows itself to any thing.*

中文 那個遊蕩的瘋子，可以去任何他想去的地方。

第四幕
第一景

●track *037*

206. despise *(vt.)* 鄙視，看不起

英文 I was reminded of my son, even though I despised my son at that time.

原句 *My son came then into my mind, and yet my mind was then scarce friends with him.*

中文 那使我想起我的兒子，雖然我那時對他沒什麼好感。

207. tragedy *(n.)* 悲劇，慘案，災難

英文 It's the tragedy of our times that lunatics must lead the blind.

原句 *Tis the time's plague when madmen lead the blind.*

中文 我們身處這悲劇的時代，瘋子必須帶著瞎子走路。

208. bleed *(vt.)* 榨取，勒索，給……抽血 (或放血)；
(vi.) 出血，流血

英文 Your dear eyes are bleeding.

原句 *Bless thy sweet eyes, they bleed.*

中文 你珍貴的眼睛流血了。

---

209. cliff *(n.)* 懸崖，峭壁

---

210. precariously *(adv.)* 不安全地，危險地

英文 There's a cliff there that leans precariously over the deep sea.

原句 *There is a cliff, whose high and bending head looks fearfully in the confinèd deep.*

中文 那邊有一座懸崖，險峻地佇立在幽深的海水旁。

多樣性解釋

　　莎士比亞的戲劇之所以經典，是因為它存在著多樣性的解釋，可謂「一百個人眼中有一百個哈姆雷特」，而這也是莎劇的魅力所在。同樣地，從現代人的眼光看李爾王，會發現生活中有太多李爾王，過多的虛榮心會導致許多不好的後果。就像李爾王是一個專橫暴虐、剛愎自用的統治者形象，他致命的錯誤便是虛榮心，身為長期處於最高統治地位，總是被人讚賞因而導致虛榮心，不習慣於小女兒的誠實和拙於言語。

●track *038*

211. mild *(adj.)* 溫和的，味淡的，輕微的

英文 I'm surprised my mild husband didn't meet me on the way here.

原句 *I marvel our mild husband not met us on the way.*

中文 我覺得很意外，我溫柔的丈夫沒有來這裏迎接我。

212. delight *(vt.)* 使高興；*(vi.)* 高興，取樂；*(n.)* 愉快，樂事

213. disgust *(vt.)* 使作嘔，使厭惡；*(n.)* 作嘔，厭惡

英文 He was delighted by the bad news and disgusted by the good news.

原句 *What most he should dislike seems pleasant to him; what like, offensive.*

中文 他應該痛恨的事情，反而讓他覺得高興；他應該欣慰的事情，卻令他厭惡。

214. appreciate *(vt.)* 欣賞，賞識，感謝；*(vi.)* 增值

英文 Bad people can't appreciate wisdom or goodness.

原句 *Wisdom and goodness to the vile seem vile.*

中文 智慧和仁義在惡人眼中看來都是惡的。

215. deform *(vt.)* 使成畸形，使變形；*(vi.)* 變畸形，變形

英文 A woman deformed by hatred and rage is more horrifying than the devil

原句 *Proper deformity shows not in the fiend so horrid as in woman.*

中文 惡魔醜惡的嘴臉，還不及一個惡魔般的女人那樣令人害怕。

● track *039*

216. overwhelm *(vt.)* 戰勝，壓倒，覆蓋，使受不了

英文 She seemed to be trying to control her emotions, which were overwhelming her.

原句 *It seemed she was a queen over her passion; who, most rebel-like, sought to be king o'er her.*

中文 她似乎極力要克制她的感情，卻還是克制不住。

217. identity *(n.)* 身分，個性，特性

英文 When I've revealed my true identity, you'll be glad you took the time to help me out.

原句 *When I am known aright you shall not grieve, lending me this acquaintance.*

中文 當知道我是什麼人以後，你決不會後悔結識並幫助過我。

●track *040*

---

218. high and low *(ph.)* 到處，各色人等，高低貴賤的人們

英文 Search high and low, in every acre of the fields, and bring him here.

原句 *Search every acre in the high-grown field, and bring him to our eye.*

中文 到各處搜尋，把他帶來這裡。

---

219. ambition *(vt.)* 有……野心，追求；*(n.)* 雄心，抱負，野心

---

220. greed *(n.)* 貪心，貪婪

英文 We're not invading England out of ambition or greed, but out of love.

原句 *No blown ambition doth our arms incite, but love—dear love!*

中文 我們進軍英格蘭並非懷著非分的野心，而是為了愛，珍貴的愛。

●track *041*

221. in person *(ph.)* 親自，本人

英文 Is he there in person?

原句 *Himself in person there?*

中文 他親自來嗎？

222. flirte *(vt.)* 輕快地擺動；*(vi.)* 調情，搖晃地移動；
(n.) 調情者

223. glance *(vt.)* 用 (眼睛) 掃視，瞥見；*(vi.) , (n.)*
一瞥，掃視

英文 And when she was here recently, she flirted with Edmund and gave him significant glances.

原句 *And at her late being here she gave strange oeillades and most speaking looks to noble Edmund.*

中文 她最近在這裡時，跟愛德蒙眉目傳情。

第四幕
第六景

●track *042*

224. trauma *(n.)* 傷口，(感情的) 創傷

225. blindness *(n.)* 盲目，無知，輕率

英文 Then your other senses must be getting worse because of the trauma of blindness.

原句 *Why, then your other senses grow imperfect by your eyes' anguish.*

中文 你因為眼睛痛，其它感官的知覺也跟著不靈敏。

226. articulate *(vt.)* , *(vi.)* , *(adj.)* 講話清楚，發音清晰

英文 I think you're more articulate.

原句 *Methinks you're better spoken.*

中文 我覺得你説話越來越清晰。

227. foot *(n.)* 英尺，腳，足

英文 Give me your hand. You're now within a foot of the cliff's edge.

原句 *Give me your hand. You are now within a foot*

中文 把你的手給我，你現在離開懸崖邊上只有一呎了。

228. wretched *(adj.)* 不幸的，悲慘的，痛苦的

英文 If you're wretched and desperate, aren't you allowed to kill yourself?

原句 *Is wretchedness deprived that benefit to end itself by death?*

中文 難道苦命的人，連自殺的權利都被剝奪了嗎？

---

229. put up with *(ph.)* 容忍，忍受

---

230. anguish *(vt.)* 使極度痛苦；*(vi.)* 感到極度痛苦；
(n.) 極度的痛苦

英文 From now on, I'll put up with my anguish until the anguish itself cries out, "Enough, enough!" and disappears.

原句 *Henceforth I'll bear bear affliction till it do cry out itself "Enough, enough," and die.*

中文 從此以後，我要忍受痛苦，直等它有一天自己喊出「夠了，夠了！」然後再撒手死去。

---

231. absurdity *(n.)* 荒謬，荒謬的言行

---

232. mix up *(ph.)* 拌和，弄混

英文 Wisdom and absurdity mixed up together! Reason in madness!

原句 *Matter and impertinency mixed! Reason in madness!*

中文 一半有理，一半荒誕！他雖然發瘋了，說出來的話卻不是完全沒有意義。

---

233. mistress *(n.)* 女主人，主婦，情婦

英文 You're a hardworking villain who'd do anything his evil mistress wanted him to.

原句 *Aserviceable villain as duteous to the vices of thy mistress as badness would desire.*

中文 一個努力討人歡心的惡人，會做邪惡情婦希望他做的事。

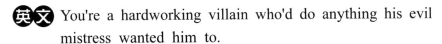

234. hallucination *(n.)* 幻覺，妄想

英文 Then my mind would be free of sorrow, and sadness would be forgotten in my hallucinations.

原句 *So should my thoughts be sever'd from my griefs and woes by wrong imaginations lose the knowledge of themselves.*

中文 然後我會擺脫懊悔的心情，憂傷也會在我的迷惘中被遺忘。

● track *043*

235. inspire *(vt.)* 鼓舞，激勵，賦予……靈感；*(vi.)* 賦予靈感

236. compassion *(n.)* 憐憫，同情

英文 If you hadn't been their father, your white hair would have inspired in them only compassion.

原句 *Had you not been their father, these white flakes had challenged pity of them.*

中文 假如你不是她們的父親，這滿頭的斑白的頭髮也應該會引起她們的憐憫。

237. senile *(adj.)* 老邁的

英文 I'm a foolish, senile old man, eighty-something years old, not an hour more or less.

原句 *I am a very foolish fond old man, fourscore and upward, not an hour more nor less.*

中文 我是一個愚蠢的老頭子，足足活了八十歲。

238. recall *(vt.)* 回想，召回，收回；*(vi.)* 記得，回想；*(n.)* 回想，召回

英文 I can't recall where I slept last night.

原句 *Nor I know not where I did lodge last night.*

中文 我想不起來昨天晚上在什麼地方過夜。

239. it's time *(ph.)* 這是……的時候

240. reassess *(vt.)* 對……再評價

英文 It's time to reassess the situation.

原句 *'Tis time to look about.*

中文 現在是應該審慎注意的時候了。

第五幕
第一景

●track *044*

---

241. be friendly with *(ph.)* 和……成為朋友

英文 I can't stand her. Please, my lord, don't be friendly with her.

原句 *I never shall endure her: dear my lord, be not familiar with her.*

中文 我不能接受她,親愛的,不要跟她要好。

---

242. come between *(ph.)* 分開,干涉,阻礙

英文 I'd rather lose this battle than allow that sister of mine to come between me and Edmund.

原句 *I had rather lose the battle than that sister should loosen him and me.*

中文 我寧願這一次戰爭失敗,也不讓我妹妹介入我和愛德蒙之間。

---

243. domestic *(adj.)* 家庭的,國家的,國內的

---

244. squabble *(vi.)* , *(n.)* 爭吵,口角

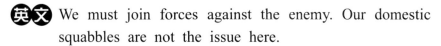

英文 We must join forces against the enemy. Our domestic squabbles are not the issue here.

原句 *Combine together 'gainst the enemy, for these domestic and particular broils are not the question here.*

中文 我們必須同心合力對抗敵人，這些內部的糾紛不是現在該討論的問題。

第五幕
第二景

●track *045*

---

245. shade *(n.)* 陰涼處，遮光物，色彩的濃淡

英文 Here, father, rest awhile in the shade of this tree.

原句 *Here, father, take the shadow of this tree*

中文 前輩，請到這樹蔭底下休息一下。

第五幕
第二景

●track *046*

---

246. get down on one's knees *(ph.)* 跪下來

英文 When you ask for my blessing, I'll get down on my knees and ask you to forgive me.

原句 *When thou dost ask me blessing, I'll kneel down and ask of thee forgiveness.*

中文 當你要求我為你祝福時，我要跪下來求你饒恕。

---

247. separate *(vt.)* 分隔，使分離；*(vi.)* 分開，脫離

---

248. togetherness *(n.)* 親密無間，和睦

英文 Anyone who wants to separate us will have to smoke us out of the cave of our togetherness like foxes.

原句 *He that parts us shall bring a brand from heaven, and fire us hence like foxes.*

中文 想分開我們的人，必須用火像驅逐狐狸出洞一樣分散我們。

---

249. scum *(n.)* 浮渣，渣滓，人渣

英文 I killed the scum who was hanging you.

原句 *I killed the slave that was a-hanging thee.*

中文 我親手殺死了那把絞死你的人渣。

---

250. disturb *(vt.)* , *(vi.)* 妨礙，打擾

英文 Don't disturb his soul. Let it go up to heaven.

原句 *Vex not his ghost. O, let him pass.*

中文 不要打擾他的靈魂。讓他安然死去吧！

劇情簡介

《馬克白》
(Macbeth)

　　蘇格蘭大將馬克白與班戈 (Banquo) 擊敗敵軍，正自戰場榮譽歸來，馬克白受封為「考特爵士」。奇怪的是，歸途中的天氣時好時壞，透露著詭異的氣氛，這時他們遇到了三名女巫，這三名女巫告訴馬克白與班戈許多預言，她們稱馬克白為「考特爵士」、「未來的國王」，並預言班戈的子孫將世代為王。兩個人對女巫的預言有著截然不同的態度，班戈懷疑女巫的動機，並認為女巫只會以部分事實來迷惑人；相反地，馬克白卻願意相信女巫的話，並在女巫消失後，受女巫這席話的鼓動，思緒翻騰不已，並將女巫的預言寫信告訴妻子。

　　蘇格蘭國王鄧肯 (Duncan) 在冊封兒子梅爾康 (Malcolm) 為王儲之後，決定造訪馬克白的城堡，為獎勵、標榜他的功勳。馬克白夫人比馬克白更有奪位掌權的野心，她得知國王鄧肯要來城堡的消息，便極力慫恿馬克白謀殺鄧肯，要他狠下心來把握良機，並策劃好殺害的

時機。馬克白深刻地知道鄧肯是個仁慈的君王，他身為臣子應該保護他，怎麼可以做出這種傷天害理的事。但終究因利慾薰心，殺害了鄧肯，而且誣賴是鄧肯的兒子為了王位，指使衛兵狠心所為。接著，鄧肯的兩個兒子梅爾康與杜納班 (Donalbain)，為了保命流亡他國，馬克白便如願稱王了。

登基後，馬克白依然無法安心，深懼班戈的子孫會如女巫的預言般搶奪自己的王權，於是又殺了班戈，但班戈的兒子逃脫了。後來馬克白去尋求女巫的協助，女巫召來三名幽靈，分別指點他三件事：小心蘇格蘭貴族麥德夫 (Macduff)、沒有女人所生的人能夠危害他以及他不會戰敗，除非勃南地區的樹林會移動位置。

聽完女巫的一席話，馬克白便信心百倍地離開了。這時，麥德夫因不滿馬克白的暴政，逃往英格蘭尋找梅爾康，密謀反叛的計畫。接著，麥德夫全家老小慘遭殺害，這個不幸的消息，傳入了麥德夫的耳裡，更堅定了他推翻馬克白的報仇決心。另一方面，馬克白夫婦殺人的罪行也被揭露出來了，因為馬克白夫人受不了精神壓力，除了有不斷洗手企圖洗掉手上血跡的異常行為，更在夢遊時說出了不為人知的惡行始末。

不久後，麥德夫所率領的軍隊砍下勃南地區的樹枝擋在身前，於是軍隊前進時就好像樹林移動位置，直到麥德夫進攻馬克白城堡近郊，心焦意亂的馬克白出城迎戰。馬克白與麥德夫單獨對戰時，心理依靠的不過是女

巫的片面預言，他始終相信女人所生的不足懼，並認為自己不會失敗，但沒想到麥德夫是剖腹生下的，並非為女人所生，這大大挫敗了馬克白的信心，使他慘死於麥德夫熱切報仇的劍下。馬克白死後，義師大獲全勝，由梅爾康續任王位。

第一幕
第一景

● track *047*

251.	thunder *(n.)* 雷，雷聲，似雷的響聲

252.	lightning *(n.)* 閃電，電光

英文 When should the three of us meet again? Will it be in thunder, lightning, or rain?

原句 *When shall we three meet again? In thunder, lightning, or in rain?*

中文 我們三個什麼時候再碰面？在打雷、閃電或下雨時？

253.	sunset *(n.)* 日落，日落景象，晚年

英文 That will happen before sunset.

原句 *That will be ere the set of sun.*

中文 那會發生在日落前。

254.	fair *(adj.)* 公正的，誠實的，美麗的；*(adv.)* 公正地，正面地

255. filthy *(adj.)* 汙穢的，卑劣的

英文 Fair is foul, and foul is fair. Let's fly away through the fog and filthy air.

原句 *Fair is foul, and foul is fair: hover through the fog and filthy air.*

中文 美即醜惡，醜即美，讓我們穿越過陰霾汙穢的空氣。

●track *048*

256. brave *(adj.)* 勇敢的，英勇的

257. capture *(vt.)* , *(n.)* 俘獲，捕獲，獲得

英文 This is the brave sergeant who fought to keep me from being captured.

原句 *This is the sergeant who like a good and hardy soldier fought 'gainst my captivity.*

中文 這就是那個奮勇救我突圍的軍官。

258. betray *(vt.)* 背叛，洩漏，透露

英文 The thane of Cawdor will never again betray me.

原句 *No more that thane of Cawdor shall deceive our bosom interest.*

中文 考特爵士再也不能騙取我的信任。

●track *049*

---

259. miserable *(adj.)* 痛苦的，不幸的，悽慘的

英文 Although I can't make his ship disappear, I can still make his journey miserable.

原句 *Though his bark cannot be lost, yet it can be tempest tossed.*

中文 雖然我不能翻覆他的船，卻可以讓他在旅程中遭遇不幸。

---

260. charm *(vt.)* 使陶醉，吸引；*(vi.)* 施魔法；*(n.)* 魅力，咒語

英文 The charm is ready.

原句 *The charm's wound up.*

中文 咒語已經生效了。

---

261. at the same time *(ph.)* 同時，一起

英文 I have never seen a day that was so good and bad at the same time.

原句 *So foul and fair a day I have not seen.*

中文 我從來沒有見過這樣既清朗又惡劣的天氣。

---

262. startle *(vt.)* 使驚嚇，使驚奇；*(vi.)* , *(n.)* 驚嚇，驚奇

英文 Why do you look so startled and afraid of these nice things they're saying?

原句 *Why do you start and seem to fear things that do sound so fair?*

中文 你為什麼如此吃驚，而且對這些她們所說的好事感到害怕？

---

263. lesser *(adj.)* 較小的，更少的，次要的；*(adv.)* 較少地

英文 You are lesser than Macbeth but also greater.

原句 *Lesser than Macbeth, and greater.*

中文 你比馬克白低微，可是你的地位在他之上。

---

264. descendant *(adj.)* 子孫，後裔；*(n.)* 祖傳的，下降的

英文 Your descendants will be kings, even though you will not be one.

原句 *Thou shalt get kings, though thou be none.*

中文 你雖然不會是君王，你的子孫們將會成為一國之君。

---

265. desolate *(adj.)* 荒蕪的，孤寂的，被遺棄的

---

266. prophetic *(adj.)* 預言的，先知的，預示的

英文 Tell me where you learned these strange things, and why you stop us at this desolate place with this prophetic greeting?

原句 *Say from whence you owe this strange intelligence, or why upon this blasted heath you stop our way with such prophetic greeting.*

中文 告訴我你們從何得知這種奇怪的消息？為什麼你們要在這荒涼的曠野攔下我們，然後說了這些預言？

267.	in order to (ph.) 為了……

268.	destruction (n.) 破壞，消滅

英文 The agents of evil often tell us part of the truth in order to lead us to our destruction.

原句 *The instruments of darkness tell us truths, win us with honest trifles, to betray 's in deepest consequence.*

中文 魔鬼往往只說出一部分的真話來誘導我們，然後讓我們陷入毀滅的結果。

最黑陰的悲劇

　　《馬克白》是莎士比亞最短的悲劇，故事的地點設在蘇格蘭，大致上根據蘇格蘭哲學家赫克托波伊斯的《蘇格蘭國王馬克白》寫成。《馬克白》經常被認為是莎士比亞悲劇中最為陰暗、最富震撼力的作品。他以戲劇的方式、通過心理作用、政治爭鬥的方式，觀察並深刻呈現出追逐權勢而背信棄義的邪惡心態。

269. execute *(vt.)* 實施，執行，將……處死

英文 Has the former thane of Cawdor been executed yet?

原句 *Is execution done on Cawdor?*

中文 前考特爵士執行死刑了嗎？

270. without equal *(ph.)* 無以倫比，難以匹敵

英文 He is a kinsman without equal.

原句 *It is a peerless kinsman.*

中文 他真是一個無以倫比的好兄弟。

271. desperately *(adj.)* 絕望地；不顧一切地，拼命地

272. vanish *(vt.)* 使不見，使消失；*(vi.)* 突然不見，消逝，絕跡

英文 When I tried desperately to question them further, they vanished into thin air.

原句 *When I burned in desire to question them further, they made themselves air, into which they vanished.*

中文 我熱切地想要再問她們問題時,她們就已經消失在空中。

---

273. seize *(vt.)* , *(vi.)* 抓住,奪取,利用

---

274. wholeheartedly *(adv.)* 全心全意地,全神貫注地

英文 You are too full of the milk of human kindness to seize this extraordinary opportunity wholeheartedly.

原句 *Yet do I fear thy nature; it is too full o' th' milk of human kindness to catch the nearest way.*

中文 你的天性充滿人性的溫情,使你不敢採取積極的行動抓住這個前所未有的機會。

---

275. witchcraft *(n.)* 巫術,魔法,魔力

英文 Fate and witchcraft both seem to want you to be a king.

原句 *Fate and metaphysical aid doth seem to have thee crown'd withal.*

中文 命運和神祕的力量似乎都希望你成為君王。

---

276. from head to toe *(ph.)* 從頭到腳,全身

---

277. deadly *(adj.)* 致命的,極度的; *(adv.)* 死一般地,極度地

---

278. cruelty *(n.)* 殘酷,殘忍,殘酷的行為

英文 Come, you spirits that assist murderous thoughts, make

me less like a woman and more like a man, and fill me from head to toe with deadly cruelty!

（原句） *Come, you spirits that tend on mortal thoughts, unsex me here and fill me from the crown to the toe top-full of direst cruelty.*

（中文）來，神靈，解除我的女性柔弱的特質，將兇惡殘忍從頭到腳貫注在我的身上。

第一幕
第六景

●track *052*

| 279. | spur *(vt.)* 用靴刺踢，鞭策，鼓勵；*(vi.)* 策馬飛奔，給予刺激；*(n.)* 踢馬刺，刺激，激勵 |

（英文）And his great love, which is as sharp as his spur, helped him beat us here.

（原句） *And his great love, sharp as his spur, hath holp him to his home before us.*

（中文）他的忠心跟他騎馬的技術一樣令人讚賞，使得他比我們先一步回來。

| 280. | favor *(vt.)* 支持，偏愛，有利於；*(n.)* 贊成，偏愛，恩惠 |

（英文）I love him dearly, and I shall continue to favor him.

（原句） *We love him highly and shall continue our graces towards him.*

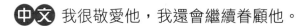

中文 我很敬愛他,我還會繼續眷顧他。

●track *053*

---

281. first of all *(ph.)* 首先,最初,首要

---

282. subject *(adj.)* 隸屬的;*(n.)* 主題,科目,臣民

英文 First of all, I am his kinsman and his subject, so I should always try to protect him.

原句 *First, as I am his kinsman and his subject, strong both against the deed,*

中文 首先,我是他的親戚,又是他的臣子,因此我應該要保護他。

---

283. opinion *(n.)* 意見,評價,輿論

英文 The king has just honored me, and I have earned the good opinion of all sorts of people.

原句 *He hath honored me of late, and I have bought golden opinions from all sorts of people.*

中文 他最近給我榮銜,而且我也贏得各領域人們的好評。

---

284. pluck *(vt.)* , *(vi.)* 拔,扯;*(n.)* 拔,扯,動物內臟,勇氣

285. smash *(vt.)* 粉碎，擊毀；*(vi.)*，*(n.)* 碎裂，猛撞，垮掉

英文 But even as the baby was smiling up at me, I would have plucked my nipple out of its mouth and smashed its brain out against a wall if I had sworn to do that the same way you have sworn to do this.

原句 *I would, while it was smiling in my face, have plucked my nipple from his boneless gums, and dashed the brains out, had I so sworn as you have done to this.*

中文 假如我也像你一樣，發誓下要做這件事，就算是懷中哺乳中的嬰兒對我微笑，我也會從它的嘴中拔出我的乳頭，然後把它的腦袋砸碎。

第二幕
第一景

● track *053*

286. in a/the mood *(ph.)* ……的心情

287. grant *(vt.)* 同意，給予，承認；*(n.)* 同意，給予，承認，獎學金

英文 He's been in an unusually good mood and has granted many gifts to your household and servants.

原句 *He hath been in unusual pleasure, and sent forth great largess to your offices.*

中文 他今天非常高興，賞了你的家人僕人許多東西。

---

288. handle *(vt.)* 操作，對待，處理；*(n.)* 柄，把手，柄狀物

英文 Is this a dagger I see in front of me, with its handle pointing toward my hand?

原句 *Is this a dagger which I see before me, the handle toward my hand?*

中文 我眼前看到柄對著我的手的那個東西，是一把刀子嗎？

---

289. splotch *(vt.)* 弄汙；*(n.)* 污漬，斑點

英文 I can still see you, and I see blood splotches on your blade and handle that weren't there before.

原句 *I see thee still, and on thy blade and dudgeon gouts of blood, which was not so before.*

中文 我還是看得到你，我看到刀上還流著一滴一滴剛才所沒有的血。

---

290. summon *(vt.)* 召喚，請求，喚起

英文 Don't listen to the bell, Duncan, because it summons you either to heaven or to hell.

原句 *Hear it not, Duncan, for it is a knell that summons thee to heaven or to hell.*

中文 不要聽那個鐘聲，鄧肯，這是召喚你上天堂或者下地獄的喪鐘。

---

291. alcohol *(n.)* 含酒精飲料，酒

英文 The alcohol that got the servants drunk has made me bold.

原句 *That which hath made them drunk hath made me bold.*

中文 讓侍衛醉倒的酒，卻提起我的勇氣。

---

292. owl *(n.)* 貓頭鷹，常熬夜的人，慣於夜間活動者

英文 I heard the owl scream and the crickets cry.

原句 *I heard the owl scream and the crickets cry.*

中文 我聽見夜梟的啼聲和蟋蟀鳴叫。

---

293. blessing (n.) 上帝的賜福，祝福，幸事

英文 I desperately needed God's blessing, but the word "Amen" stuck in my throat.

原句 *I had most need of blessing, and "Amen" stuck in my throat.*

中文 我迫切需要上帝垂恩幫助，可是「阿門」兩個字卻哽在我的喉頭。

---

294. smear *(vt.)* 塗抹，弄髒，誹謗；*(vi.)* 被弄髒；*(n.)* 汙跡，誹謗

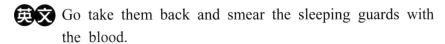

英文 Go take them back and smear the sleeping guards with the blood.

原句 *Go carry them and smear the sleepy grooms with blood.*

中文 把它們拿回去，塗一些血在那兩個熟睡的侍衛身上。

---

295. guilt (n.) 犯罪，過失，內疚

英文 A little water will wash away the evidence of our guilt. It's so simple!

原句 *A little water clears us of this deed. How easy is it, then!*

中文 一點點的水就可以把我們犯罪的證據清洗乾淨，那是多麼容易的事！

豆知識

以穿衣巧喻野心

　　《馬克白》中的重要主題是：當野心超越道德束縛時，所造成的毀滅與破壞。馬克白本是有功勳的英雄，性格中有善和美的一面，但因為王位的誘惑和野心的驅使，最後淪為血腥殺人、懊悔無及的罪人。他野心勃勃地渴望權勢，使他棄絕了的理性判斷，殺死了國王，陷入了內疚與偏執當中。莎士比亞巧妙地以穿錯衣服來暗喻他不洽當的野心，讓他醜態百出，例如：「他的衣服不是太大就是太小——好比他的野心太大，而他真當了王卻一塌糊塗。」

● track *055*

---

296. chaotic *(adj.)* 混亂的，雜亂無章的，無秩序的

英文 The night has been chaotic.

原句 *The night has been unruly.*

中文 這一夜一直不平靜。

---

297. renowned *(adj.)* 有名的，有聲譽的

英文 The graceful and renowned king is dead.

原句 *Renown and grace is dead.*

中文 仁慈又聲名卓著的國王死了。

---

298. splatter *(vt.)* , *(vi.)* 濺潑；*(n.)* 濺出物

---

299. precious *(adj.)* 貴重的，珍貴的，寶貝的；*(n.)* 心愛的人

英文 There was Duncan, and his white skin all splattered with his precious blood.

原句 *Here lay Duncan, his silver skin laced with his golden blood.*

中文 這兒躺著鄧肯，他白色的皮膚流淌著他珍貴的血。

---

300. take care of *(ph.)* 照顧，留意，處理

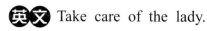 Take care of the lady.

原句 *Look to the lady.*

中文 照顧一下夫人。

---

301. keep quiet (使) 保持安靜，滿足，無怨言

---

302. have the most to say *(ph.)* 最有發言的資格，
最有發言的關聯性

英文 Why are we keeping quiet? The two of us have the most to say in this matter.

原句 *Why do we hold our tongues, that most may claim this argument for ours?*

中文 我們為什麼一言不發？這件事和我們最有關係。

---

303. weep *(vt.)* , *(vi.)* , *(n.)* 哭泣，流淚

英文 We haven't even begun to weep yet.

原句 *Our tears are not yet brewed.*

中文 我們深重的悲哀甚至還沒有開始。

第一幕
第四景

● track *056*

---

304. commit *(vt.)* 犯罪，做錯事，把⋯⋯交託給

英文 It's unnatural, just like the murder that has been committed.

(原句) *'Tis unnatural, Even like the deed that's done.*

(中文) 這種現象很反常，正像那件驚人的謀殺案一樣。

---

305. go with *(ph.)* 相合，同意，和……為伴

(英文) May God's blessing go with you and with all who turn bad into good, and enemies into friends!

(原句) *God's benison go with you and with those that would make good of bad and friends of foes.*

(中文) 願上帝祝福你，也祝福那些把惡事化成善事，把仇敵化成朋友的人們。

●track *057*

---

306. suspect *(vt.)* 懷疑，察覺，猜想；*(vi.)* 懷疑，疑心

---

307. cheat *(vt.)* 欺騙，詐取；*(vi.)* 行騙，作弊，不貞；
(n.) 欺詐，作弊

英文 I suspect you cheated to win these titles.

原句 *I fear thou played'st most foully for 't.*

中文 我懷疑你用欺騙的手段得到這些名位。

---

308. ceremonial *(adj.)* 禮節的，儀式的，正式的 *(n.)*
禮節，禮俗，儀式

莎劇中最厭女的作品

　　因為馬克白這個角色的罪惡來自於女性，一些評論家因此辯稱《馬克白》是莎劇中最為厭女的作品。儘管劇中的男性角色和女性角色一樣邪惡，但女性角色之所以可惡得驚人，是因為她們的行為與社會的期望大相逕庭。馬克白夫人的行為充分顯現女性的野心與殘忍上絕不遜於男性，或許是出於社會對其性別的制約，也或許是她的膽量不足，馬克白夫人才會採用通過擺佈她的丈夫來達到自己的目的。

309. banquet *(vt.)* 宴請；*(vi.)* 參加宴會；*(n.)*
宴會，宴請，款待

英文 Tonight we're having a ceremonial banquet, and I want you to be there.

原句 *Tonight we hold a solemn supper, Sir, and I'll request your presence.*

中文 我們今天晚上要舉行盛宴，請你務必出席。

310. feast *(vt.)* 盛宴款待；*(vi.)* 參加宴會，享受；
(n.) 盛宴，筵席

英文 Don't miss our feast.

原句 *Fail not our feast.*

中文 不要錯過我們的宴會。

311. hit the road *(ph.)* 上路，出發

英文 It's time we hit the road.

原句 *Our time does call upon 's.*

中文 是我們該上路的時候了。

312. enjoyable *(adj.)* 快樂的，有樂趣的

英文 In order to make your company even more enjoyable, I'm going to keep to myself until suppertime.

原句 *To make society the sweeter welcome, we will keep ourself till supper-time alone.*

中文 為了能夠更加感受到各位嘉賓相伴的快樂，我在晚餐以前先獨處一下。

313.　**get rid of** *(ph.)* 擺脫

英文 I will tell you a plan that will get rid of your enemy and bring you closer to me.

原句 *I will put that business in your bosoms, grapples you to the heart and love of us*

中文 我要告訴你一個計畫,可以除去你們的仇人,而且還可以討我歡心。

314.　**determination** *(n.)* 堅定,果斷,決心

英文 I can see the determination in your eyes.

原句 *Your spirits shine through you.*

中文 你們的眼睛已經充分流露出決心。

●track *058*

315.　**fix it** *(ph.)* 修補

316.　**a second thought** *(ph.)* 改變想法,重新考慮

英文 If you can't fix it, you shouldn't give it a second thought. What's done is done.

原句 *Things without all remedy should be without regard. What's done is done.*

中文 假如是無法挽回的事,就不要再去想,事情做了就算了。

317. endure *(vt.)* 忍耐，容忍；*(vi.)* 忍耐，持久

318. deprivation *(n.)* 剝奪，免職

英文 I'd rather be dead than endure this endless mental torture and harrowing sleep deprivation.

原句 *Better be with the dead. Whom we, to gain our peace, have sent to peace, Than on the torture of the mind to lie.*

中文 我寧願死掉，也不要忍受永無止盡的精神折磨和痛苦的失眠。

319. deed *(n.)* 行為，功績，證書

英文 Bad deeds force you to commit more bad deeds.

原句 *Things bad begun make strong themselves by ill.*

中文 以不義開始的事情，會使你犯下更多的罪惡。

第三幕
第二景

• track *059*

320. the rest of *(n.)* 剩餘部分，其餘的人

英文 The rest of the king's guests are already inside.

原句 *The rest that are within the note of expectation already are i' th' court.*

中文 其餘的賓客都已經在屋內了。

321. accomplish *(vt.)* 完成，實現，達到

英文 Well, let's get out of here and tell the king what we did accomplish.

原句 *Well, let's away and say how much is done.*

中文 好，我們回去報告我們的行動結果。

● track *060*

322. rank *(vt.)* 把……排成行；*(vi.)* 列為，列隊；
(n.) 等級，社會階層，軍階

英文 You know your own ranks, so you know where to sit.

原句 *You know your own degrees; sit down.*

中文 大家按著個人自己的階級入座。

323. mingle *(vt.)* 使混合；*(vi.)* 混合起來

324. humble *(vt.)* 使謙卑，使地位降低；*(adj.)* 謙遜的，
地位低下的

英文 I will walk around and mingle with all of you, playing the humble host.

原句 *Ourself will mingle with society and play the humble host.*

中文 我會跟你們在一起，扮演一個謙恭的主人。

325.	ditch *(vt.)* 在……上掘溝，丟棄；*(vi.)* 掘溝；*(n.)* 溝，壕溝

326.	gash *(vt.)* 砍傷，劃開；*(n.)* 深長的傷口，地面上的裂縫

英文 He's lying dead in a ditch, with twenty deep gashes in his head, the least one of which would have been enough to kill him.

原句 *Safe in a ditch he bides, with twenty trenchèd gashes on his head, the least a death to nature.*

中文 他已經躺在壕溝裏，頭上有二十道傷口，最輕的一道就足以使他致命。

327.	It's nice of you to... *(ph.)* 你……真是太好了

英文 It's nice of you to remind me.

原句 *Sweet remembrancer!*

中文 還好你提醒了我。

328.	pay attention to *(ph.)* 關心，注意

英文 Eat your dinner and pay no attention to him.

原句 *Feed and regard him not.*

中文 儘管吃喝，不要太在意他！

329.	inexperience *(adj.)* 無經驗，不諳世故，不熟練

英文 My strange self-delusions just come from inexperience.

原句 *My strange and self-abuse is the initiate fear that wants hard use.*

中文 我會產生奇怪的妄想，是因為我們缺少做這種事的經驗。

第三幕
第五景

● track *061*

---

330. disobedient *(adj.)* 不服從的，違抗命令的，違反規則的

英文 Don't I have a reason to be angry, you disobedient hags?

原句 *Have I not reason, beldams as you are?*

中文 我沒有理由對你們這些放肆的醜婆子生氣嗎？

---

331. overconfidence *(n.)* 自負

英文 As you all know, overconfidence is man's greatest enemy.

原句 *And you all know, security is mortals' chiefest enemy.*

中文 你們都知道，自信是人類最大的仇敵。

第三幕
第六景

● track *062*

---

332. alike *(adj.)* 相同的，相像的；*(adv.)* 一樣地，相似地

333. draw a conclusion *(ph.)* 得出結論

英文 What I've already said shows you we think alike, so you can draw your own conclusions.

原句 *My former speeches have but hit your thoughts, which can interpret farther.*

中文 我所說的是要讓你知道我們的想法一樣，所以，現在你可以進一步說出你的推論。

334. pine for *(ph.)* 渴望，十分盼望

英文 Those are the things we pine for now.

原句 *All which we pine for now.*

中文 這一切都是我們現在渴望得到的。

335. regret *(vt.)* 懊悔，因……而遺憾，為……抱歉；*(vi.)* 感到後悔，感到抱歉；*(n.)* 懊悔，抱歉，遺憾

英文 You'll regret the day you gave me this answer.

原句 *You'll rue the time that clogs me with this answer.*

中文 你有一天會後悔你這樣回答我。

●track *063*

336. effort *(n.)* 努力，盡力，努力的成果

英文 I admire your efforts, and all of you will share the rewards.

原句 *I commend your pains, and every one shall share i' th' gains.*

中文 辛苦你們了，大家都能分到好處。

---

337. cauldron *(n.)* 大鍋

英文 Now come sing around the cauldron like a ring of elves and fairies, enchanting everything you put in.

原句 *And now about the cauldron sing, like elves and fairies in a ring, enchanting all that you put in.*

中文 現在圍著鍋邊像精靈一樣跳舞，對你們放進鍋內的東西施以魔法。

---

338. reign *(vi.)* 統治；*(n.)* 統治，支配，統治時期

英文 Tell me, if your dark powers can see this far: will Banquo's sons ever reign in this kingdom?

原句 *Tell me, if your art can tell so much: shall Banquo's issue ever reign in this kingdom?*

中文 假如你們的魔法能夠解答我的疑問，告訴我：班柯的子孫們會不會統治這個王國？

● track *064*

---

339. traitor *(n.)* 叛徒，叛國者，賣國賊

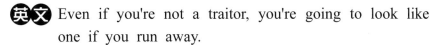

英文 Even if you're not a traitor, you're going to look like one if you run away.

原句 *When our actions do not, our fears do make us traitors.*

中文 就算你不是叛徒，但只要你逃跑，反而看起來成了叛徒。

---

340. disreputable *(adj.)* 聲名狼藉的，不光彩的

---

341. thug *(n.)* 惡棍，刺客，暴徒

英文 I hope he's not anywhere so disreputable that thugs like you can find him.

原句 *I hope, in no place so unsanctified where such as thou mayst find him.*

中文 我希望他現在逃到正派光明的地方，好讓你們這些惡棍不敢露臉抓他。

● track *065*

---

342. shady *(adj.)* 成蔭的，陰暗的，名聲不好的

英文 Let's seek out some shady place where we can sit down alone and cry our hearts out.

原句 *Let us seek out some desolate shade and there weep our sad bosoms empty.*

中文 讓我們找一處隱蔽的地方，然後坐下來痛快哭一場。

343. tyrant *(n.)* 暴君，專橫的人

英文 This tyrant, whose mere name is so awful it hurts us to say it, was once considered an honest man.

原句 *This tyrant, whose sole name blisters our tongues, was once thought honest.*

中文 這個暴君的名字現在讓我們痛斥，可是他曾經擁有正直的名聲。

344. downfall *(n.)* 墜落，沒落，大陣雨 (或雪)

英文 Endless greed and lust in a man's nature is a kind of tyranny. It has caused the downfall of many kings

原句 *It hath been the untimely emptying of the happy throne and fall of many kings.*

中文 永無止盡的貪婪和欲望是一種暴政，它已經使無數君主沒落。

345. savagely *(adv.)* 野蠻地，殘暴地，猛烈地

英文 Your castle was attacked. Your wife and children were savagely slaughtered.

原句 *Your castle is surprised, your wife and babes savagely slaughtered.*

中文 你的城堡遭受襲擊，你的妻兒也都慘死於野蠻的殺戮。

●track 066

346. stay up *(ph.)* 熬夜，處於原位不動

英文 I've stayed up with you for two nights now, and I haven't seen any evidence of what you were talking about.

原句 *I have two nights watched with you but can perceive no truth in your report.*

中文 我已經陪著你看守了兩夜，可是一點不能證實你説的事。

347. next to *(ph.)* 在……旁邊，緊鄰著，幾乎

英文 She always has to have a light next to her. Those are her orders.

原句 *She has light by her continually. 'Tis her command.*

中文 她的身旁永遠點著燭火，這是她的命令。

348. rub *(vt.)* 擦，磨擦，使相擦；*(vi.)* 磨擦，被擦掉；
(n.) 擦，摩擦

英文 Look how she rubs her hands.

原句 *Look, how she rubs her hands.*

中文 注意她如何摩擦她的手。

349. spot *(vt.)* 使沾上汙點，弄髒；*(vi.)* 沾上汙漬，
產生汙漬；*(n.)* 斑點，汙點，場所

英文 There's still a spot here.

原句 *Yet here's a spot.*

中文 但是這兒還有一點血跡。

350. keep a secret *(ph.)* 保守祕密

英文 Heaven knows what secrets she's keeping.

原句 *Heaven knows what she has known.*

中文 上天知道她內心的祕密。

351. smell *(vt.)* 嗅，聞，發出……的氣味；*(vi.)* 嗅，聞，有臭味；*(n.)* 氣味，香味，臭味，嗅覺

英文 I still have the smell of blood on my hand.

原句 *Here's the smell of the blood still.*

中文 我的手上還是有一股血腥味。

352. priest *(n.)* 牧師，神父，神職人員，祭司

英文 She needs a priest more than a doctor.

原句 *More needs she the divine than the physician.*

中文 她需要教士甚過醫生。

● track *067*

353. a list of *(ph.)* 一份……的清單，一系列的……

英文 I have a list of all the important men.

原句 *I have a file of all the gentry.*

中文 我有一張重要人物的名單。

---

354. treachery *(n.)* 背叛，變節，背信

英文 Now, rebel armies punish him every minute for his treachery.

原句 *Now minutely revolts upbraid his faith-breach.*

中文 討伐軍隊分分秒秒，都在責罰他的不忠不義。

---

355. deserve *(vt.)* 應受，該得；*(vi.)* 應受賞 (罰)

英文 Well, let's keep marching and give our loyalty to someone who truly deserves it.

原句 *Well, march we on, to give obedience where 'tis truly owed.*

中文 好，我們不斷前進，而且效忠真正值得我們忠心對待的人。

第五幕
第三景

● track *068*

---

356. defeat *(vt.)* 戰勝，擊敗，使失敗；*(n.)* 失敗，擊敗

英文 Don't be afraid, Macbeth. No man born from a woman will ever defeat you.

原句 *Fear not, Macbeth. No man that's born of woman shall e'er have power upon thee.*

中文 不要害怕，馬克白，沒有一個婦人所生下的人可以加害於你。

357. wither *(vt.)* 使枯萎，使凋謝，使衰亡；*(vi.)* 枯萎，
凋謝，失去生氣

英文 The course of my life is beginning to wither and fall away, like a yellowing leaf.

原句 *My way of life is fall'n into the sere, the yellow leaf.*

中文 我的生命已經漸漸枯萎，像一片凋落的黃葉。

358. vision *(vt.)* 夢見，在幻覺中看見；*(n.)* 視力，
洞察力，幻覺，夢想

英文 She is troubled with endless visions that keep her from sleeping.

原句 *She is troubled with thick-coming fancies that keep her from her rest.*

中文 她因為不斷出現幻覺，使得她無法睡眠。

豆知識
比叛亂更可怕的女巫

　　在莎士比亞時期，女巫被認為比叛亂更為可惡，《馬克白》劇中的三位女巫代表了黑暗、混亂、爭鬥，她們的出現代表了背叛與毀滅。她們不但是政治上的叛徒，更是靈魂的叛徒。許多混亂都是由於她們可以在現實與超自然之間來回穿行所致。她們任性而為，以至於無法確定是她們控制了命運，抑或只是命運的使者；她們蔑視邏輯，不受現實世界的控制，使得劇中充滿了錯亂，將邪惡誤認為良善，將良善卻誤認為是邪惡。

●track *069*

---

359. branch *(n.)* 樹枝，支流，分公司

英文 Tell every soldier to break off a branch and hold it in front of him.

原句 *Let every soldier hew him down a bough and bear't before him.*

中文 讓每一個兵士砍下一根樹枝，把它舉在每個人的前方。

---

360. conceal *(vt.)* 隱蔽，隱藏，隱瞞

---

361. inaccurate *(adj.)* 不正確的，不精確的

英文 That way we can conceal how many of us there are, and Macbeth's spies will give him inaccurate reports.

原句 *Thereby shall we shadow the numbers of our host and make discovery err in report of us.*

中文 這樣我們可以隱匿我們全軍的人數，讓敵人錯判我們的戰力。

第五幕
第五景

●track *070*

362. laugh off *(ph.)* 用笑驅除，對……一笑置之

363. seige

英文 Our castle is strong enough to laugh off their seige.

原句 *Our castle's strength will laugh a siege to scorn*

中文 我們的的城堡堅固難以摧毀，可以在笑聲中對付他們的圍攻。

364. nothing but *(ph.)* 僅僅，只有，只不過

英文 Out, out, brief candle. Life is nothing but a walking shadow.

原句 *Out, out, brief candle! Life's but a walking shadow.*

中文 滅了吧，滅了吧，短促的燭光！人生不過是一個行走的影子。

365. signify *(vt.)* 表示，意味著，預示

英文 Life is a story told by an idiot, full of sound and fury, signifying nothing.

原句 *It is a tale told by an idiot, full of sound and fury, signifying nothing.*

中文 人生是一個愚人所講的故事，充滿著喧嘩和騷動，卻毫無意義。

366. armor *(vt.)* 為⋯⋯穿盔甲；*(n.)* 盔甲

英文 At least we'll die with our armor on.

原句 *At least we'll die with harness on our back.*

中文 無論如何，死的時候也要穿著盔甲，戰死在沙場上。

●track *070*

367. throw down *(ph.)* 扔掉，拒絕，摧毀

英文 Throw down these branches and show them who you really are.

原句 *Your leafy screens throw down, and show like those you are.*

中文 仍掉你們樹枝，顯現出你們實際的隊伍。

●track *071*

368. haunt *(vt.)* 鬼魂等常出沒於，縈繞在心頭，使困擾

英文 If someone other than me kills you, the ghosts of my wife and children will haunt me forever.

原句 *If thou beest slain, and with no stroke of mine, my wife and children's ghosts will haunt me still.*

中文 如果你不能死在我的手下，那麼我妻兒的陰魂一定永遠不會放過我。

369. avoid *(vt.)* 避開，躲開，避免

英文 You are the only man I have avoided.

原句 *Of all men else I have avoided thee.*

中文 所有人當中，我唯獨最不願意看見你。

370. guilty *(adj.)* 有罪的，有過失的，內疚的

英文 I'm already guilty of killing your whole family.

原句 *My soul is too much charged with blood of thine already.*

中文 我因為殺了你們全家而有罪。

371. curse *(vt.)* , *(vi.)* , *(n.)* 詛咒，咒罵

372. frighten away *(ph.)* 嚇走

英文 Curse you for telling me this. You've frightened away my courage.

原句 *Accursèd be that tongue that tells me so, for it hath cowed my better part of man!*

中文 詛咒你告訴我這些話，讓我失去了膽量。

373. survive *(vt.)* 從……中逃生； *(vi.)* 活下來，倖存，殘留

英文 I wish all of our friends could have survived this battle.

原句 *I would the friends we miss were safe arrived.*

中文 我希望所有的朋友都能從戰場上活下來。

374.	the dawn of *(ph.)* 開端，曙光，端倪

375.	exile *(vt.)* , *(n.)* 流放，放逐，離鄉背井

英文 We have a lot to do at the dawn of this new era. We must call home all of our exiled friends who fled from the grip of tyranny.

原句 *What's more to do, which would be planted newly with the time, as calling home our exiled friends abroad that fled the snares of watchful tyranny.*

中文 在這個嶄新的時刻，我們還有許多事情要做。我們必須將那些因為逃避暴政而逃亡的朋友們召喚回來。

劇情簡介

《奧賽羅》
(Othello)

　　威尼斯德高望重的元老布拉班修 (Brabantio)，有個美麗的女兒德絲苔蒙娜 (Desdemona)，她和父親的朋友摩爾族的黑人將軍奧賽羅互相愛慕、私訂終身。

　　某天夜裡，奧賽羅的屬下伊阿高 (Iago)，夥同曾經追求過苔絲狄蒙娜的威尼斯紳士洛德里格 (Roderigo) 來到布拉班修家樓下，故意將奧賽羅與苔絲狄蒙娜互訂終身的事告訴布拉班修，布拉班修便前往議事廳向公爵控訴奧賽羅引誘他的女兒。公爵聽完奧賽羅夫婦講述他們相愛的過程後，勸布拉班修接受他們結婚的事實，這個時候，恰巧傳來賽浦路斯戰事吃緊的消息，公爵便將去賽浦路斯征服土耳其人的重責大任交給奧賽羅。

　　由於伊阿高對奧賽羅沒有提拔他做副將一事，內心始終懷恨不已，因此不斷想找機會洩恨。如今眼見挑撥失敗，內心憤恨的火燄便燃燒得更熾烈了，於是他又心生更狠毒的計謀。奧賽羅的軍隊才出征不久，就聽說敵

軍土耳其的船艦因為大風浪而被吹散。大夥兒便在賽浦路斯島守將蒙泰諾 (Montano) 的歡迎下，陸續登島休息。

在所有的朋友中，奧賽羅只信任凱西歐 (Cassio)，因為凱西歐曾經幫奧賽羅送情書給苔絲狄蒙娜，他知道奧賽羅的一切。伊阿高討厭奧賽羅拔擢凱西歐為副將，於是便在慶祝土耳其大敗的餐宴上，刻意引誘凱西歐喝酒，然後安排洛德里格挑釁凱西歐，守將蒙泰諾前來調解，卻因此被喝醉酒的凱西歐所傷，後來奧賽羅只好先解除凱西歐的官階，給蒙泰諾一個交代。接著，凱西歐在伊阿高的慫恿下，決定去找苔絲狄蒙娜替他說情，想藉此挽回被免職的處份。苔絲狄蒙娜則念著過去的情誼，答應了凱西歐的請託，去向奧賽羅求情。不過，這一切其實都是伊阿高的算計……

緊接著，伊阿高便煽動奧賽羅，讓奧賽羅懷疑苔絲狄蒙娜與凱西歐有染。不久之後，伊阿高從妻子愛蜜莉雅 (Emilia) 手中取得了奧賽羅送給苔絲狄蒙娜的訂情手帕。然後，伊阿高將手帕丟在凱西歐必經之處，讓凱西歐撿去，並告訴奧賽羅曾見到苔絲狄蒙娜用那條手帕替凱西歐擦臉。

奧賽羅為了求證要求妻子拿出訂情的手帕，因為苔絲狄蒙娜無法拿出，奧賽羅對她的懷疑變得更為堅定了。最後奧賽羅在妒火中燒的情況下，用枕頭悶死苔絲狄蒙娜。苔絲狄蒙娜死了之後，愛蜜莉雅一再追問奧賽羅的動機，奧賽羅說出了他的「嫉妒」與「證實」之後，愛

蜜莉雅大為吃驚，一切竟然只是為了那條她無意中撿到的手帕。她急忙解釋手帕被伊阿高拿去利用的事實。至此，一切陰謀水落石出。奧賽羅終於明白苔絲狄蒙娜的忠貞，但大錯已經鑄成，於是以劍自刎，了斷自己的生命。

●track *072*

---

376. find out *(ph.)* 找出，發現，查明

英文 If you find out I did, you can go ahead and hate me.

原句 *If ever I did dream of such a matter, abhor me.*

中文 如果你發現我本來就知道這件事，就隨便你去憎恨我。

---

377. military *(adj.)* 軍事的，軍用的；*(n.)* 軍人，軍隊

---

378. theory *(n.)* 學說，理論，意見

英文 His military understanding is all theory, no practice.

原句 *Mere prattle without practice is all his soldiership.*

中文 他對軍事的瞭解都只是空談，一點也不切實際。

---

379. accountant *(n.)* 會計人員，會計師

英文 This accountant is now lieutenant, while I end up as the Moor's flag-bearer.

原句 *This counter-caster, he, in good time, must his lieu-tenant be, and I—bless the mark!—, his Moorship's ancient.*

中文 這個管帳的人居然成為他的副將，而我卻只這位摩爾人旗下的一名旗手。

380.　executioner *(n.)* 劊子手，死刑執行者

英文 By God, I'd rather be his executioner.

原句 *By heaven, I rather would have been his hangman.*

中文 老天，我還寧願成為他的劊子手。

381.　promote *(vt.)* 晉升，促進，使升級

英文 That's the curse of military service. You get promoted when someone likes you, not because you're next in line.

原句 *'Tis the curse of service, preferment goes by letter and affection, not by old gradation, where each second. Stood heir to th' first.*

中文 從軍就是這麼不公平，你只要能夠得到上司的歡心就可以升遷，而不是依照資格的順序來拔擢。

382.　plainly *(adv.)* 清楚地，坦率地，簡樸地

英文 I've already told you quite plainly that my daughter will never marry you.

原句 *In honest plainness thou hast heard me say. My daughter is not for thee.*

中文 我已經坦白告訴過你，我的女兒不會跟你結婚。

383. remote *(adj.)* 遙遠的，偏僻的，久遠的

英文 This is Venice. My house isn't in some remote countryside.

原句 *This is Venice, my house is not a grange.*

中文 這裡可是威尼斯，我家並不是位在遙遠的鄉間。

384. relative *(adj.)* 相對的，比較的，相關的；*(n.)* 親戚，親屬

英文 Get me more candles, and wake up all my relatives.

原句 *Get more tapers, Raise all my kindred.*

中文 再拿些蠟燭來，叫醒所有的親族！

豆 知識
種族歧視造成悲劇

《奧賽羅》是多主題的作品，包括：愛情與嫉妒、輕信與背信、異族通婚的主題等。種族歧視是造成奧賽羅悲劇的原因之一，他本性的迷失和種族歧視有著密切聯繫，正是由於世俗的種族歧視和伊阿高的奸計，因此奧賽羅對於自己——個摩爾人、一個為平常人所害怕的人是否能真正贏得白人姑娘的愛產生懷疑，漸漸失去信心。他由堅信妻子的忠貞到懷疑其貞潔與愛，到最後完全否認她的愛情，進而殺了她，造成了倆人的悲劇。

●track 073

385. warship (n.) 軍艦，艦艇

386. one after another (ph.) 一個接一個

英文 The warships have sent a dozen messagers tonight, one after another, and many of the senators have been awakened and are at the Duke's mansion already.

原句 *The galleys have sent a dozen sequent messengers this very night at one another's heels, and many of the consuls, raised and met, are at the Duke's already.*

中文 今晚戰船已經連續不斷派使者來，許多元老都被叫醒，在公爵府裡集合了。

387. put away (ph.) 歸位，拋棄，放棄

388. rusty (adj.) 生鏽的，赭色的，生硬的

英文 Put away your bright swords. They'll get rusty in the dew.

原句 *Keep up your bright swords, for the dew will rust them.*

中文 收起你們光亮的劍，它們沾了露水會生銹的。

389. spell (vt.) 拼寫；(n.) 咒語，著魔

英文 You devil, you've put a spell on her!

原句 *Damned as thou art, thou hast enchanted her!*

中文 你這奸人，竟用妖術蠱惑她。

390. heathen *(adj.)* 異教徒的；*(n.)* 異教徒

英文 If we let crimes like this happen, slaves and heathens will be our rulers.

原句 *For if such actions may have passage free,. Bond-slaves and pagans shall our statesmen be.*

中文 如果這樣的行為可以放縱不管，奴隸和異教徒就會來領導我們。

●track *074*

391. inconsistent *(adj.)* 不一致的，不協調的，前後矛盾的

英文 These reports are inconsistent. You can't trust them.

原句 *There's no composition in this news that gives them credit.*

中文 這些消息互相矛盾，你不要相信。

392. head for *(ph.)* 向……走去，朝……移動

英文 No, I think we can be confident that the Turks aren't really headed for Rhodes.

原句 *Nay, in all confidence, he's not for Rhodes.*

中文 不，我敢説土耳其人的目標決不是羅德斯島。

393. obedient *(adj.)* 服從的，順從的，恭順的

394. blush *(vt.)* 紅著臉表示；*(vi.)* 臉紅，感到慚愧，
發窘；*(n.)* 臉紅，羞愧

英文 She's a good girl, quiet and obedient. She blushes at the slightest thing.

原句 *A maiden never bold; of spirit so still and quiet, that her motion blushed at herself.*

中文 她是一個文靜恭順的女孩子，甚至為了很小的事情，也會羞愧得滿臉通紅。

395. make a mistake *(ph.)* 犯錯，產生誤解

英文 You'd have to be stupid to think that someone so perfect could make such an unnatural mistake as that.

原句 *It is a judgment maimed and most imperfect that will confess perfection so could err.*

中文 假如你認為這樣完美的人會犯下如此不近情理的錯，那麼你的判斷就太不智了

396. invite *(vt.)* 邀請，招待，引起

397. continually *(adv.)* 不停地，屢屢地

英文 Her father loved me and used to invite me to his house often, continually asking me about my life and all the battles I've fought.

原句 *Her father loved me, oft invited me, still questioned me the story of my life from year to year, the battles, sieges, fortunes that I have passed.*

中文 她的父親很喜歡我，常常邀請我到他家，總是問起我的生活和參戰的事。

---

398. hint *(vt.)*, *(vi.)* 暗示，示意；*(n.)* 暗示，少許

---

399. emotion

英文 I took the hint and spoke to her. She said she loved me for the dangers I'd survived, and I loved her for feeling such strong emotions about me.

原句 *Upon this hint I spake: she loved me for the dangers I had passed, and I loved her that she did pity them.*

中文 我聽了這個暗示，才向她吐露我的愛意。她為了我所經歷的種種危險而愛我，我為了她對我所抱的同情而愛她。

---

400. adopt *(vt.)* 採取，收養；*(vi.)* 過繼

英文 I'd rather adopt a child than have one of my own.

原句 *I had rather to adopt a child than get it.*

中文 我寧願領養小孩，也不要自己生。

---

401. put a damper on *(ph.)* 使……受到抑制，減弱

---

402. expedition *(n.)* 遠征，探險，遠征隊

英文 So I'll have to ask you to put a damper on your marriage celebrations and take part in this dangerous expedition.

原句 *You must therefore be content to slubber the gloss of your new fortunes with this more stubborn and boist'rous expedition.*

中文 所以我要打擾你享受新婚的快樂,讓你參與這趟危險的遠征。

---

403. a tight schedule *(ph.)* 安排緊湊

英文 We're on a tight schedule.

原句 *We must obey the time.*

中文 我們要抓緊時間。

---

404. be up to *(ph.)* 視為某人的責任,勝任,忙於

英文 What we are is up to us.

原句 *'Tis in ourselves that we are thus or thus.*

中文 我們會變成怎麼樣,在於我們自己的決定。

---

405. intimate *(adj.)* 親密的,熟悉的,私人的;*(n.)* 至交,密友

英文 After a while, I'll start telling Othello that Cassio is too intimate with his wife.

原句 *After some time, to abuse Othello's ear that he is too familiar with his wife.*

中文 過一些時候,我再去告訴奧瑟羅,說凱西歐跟他的妻子太親近了。

第一幕
第一景

● track *075*

---

406. harbor *(vt.)* 庇護，藏匿； *(vi.)* 船入港停泊，躲藏；
(n.) 港灣，避難所，避風港

英文 If the Turkish fleet isn't protected in some harbor, their men must all be drowned.

原句 *If that the Turkish fleet be not ensheltered and embayed, they are drowned.*

中文 要是土耳其艦隊沒有躲進海港裡，他們早就全部沉沒了。

---

407. terrible *(adj.)* 可怕的，嚴重的，非常討厭的

---

408. badly *(adv.)* 拙劣地，邪惡地，嚴重地，非常地

英文 This terrible storm has smashed the Turks so badly that their plans are ruined.

原句 *The desperate tempest hath so banged the Turks that their designment halts.*

中文 這場風暴嚴重打擊土耳其人，使得他們無法達成進攻計畫。

---

409. governor *(n.)* 地方行政長官，州長，老板

英文 He'll be a good governor.

原句 'Tis a worthy governor.

中文 他會是個有作為的長官。

410. during (prep.) 在……的整個期間，在……的某一段時間

英文 The two of them were separated during the storm.

原句 For they were parted with foul and violent tempest.

中文 他們在風暴中分散了。

411. lost sight of (ph.) 看不見，忘掉，忽略

英文 I hope heaven protects him from the weather, because I lost sight of him on the stormy sea.

原句 Oh, let the heavens give him defense against the elements, For I have lost him on a dangerous sea.

中文 但願上天幫助他戰勝風浪，因為我們在險惡的波濤中失散了。

412. sturdy (adj.) 健壯的，堅固的，堅決的

英文 Is his ship sturdy?

原句 Is he well shipped?

中文 他的船堅固嗎？

413. stupidity (n.) 愚蠢，愚行，蠢話

414. attractive (adj.) 有吸引力的，漂亮的，動聽的

英文 No pretty woman is stupid, because her stupidity will make her more attractive to men.

原句 *She never yet was foolish that was fair, for even her folly helped her to an heir.*

中文 是美女就不會愚蠢，因為她的愚蠢會使得她對男人更具有吸引力。

---

415. not know a thing *(ph.)* 沒見識，不清楚，不知道

---

416. praise *(vt.)* , *(n.)* 稱讚，讚揚

英文 You don't know a thing! You give your best praise to the worst women.

原句 *Oh, heavy ignorance! Thou praisest the worst best.*

中文 你好沒見識，把最好的讚美給了最壞的女人。

具深意的改編

　　評論家公認《奧賽羅》取材於義大利作家卿齊歐的小說《威尼斯的摩爾人》，不過，莎士比亞進行了重大改編。其中最有深意的改編是：在卿齊歐的小說中，男主人公是個野蠻的摩爾人，他用裝滿沙子的長統襪把苔絲狄蒙娜活活打死，並偽裝現場企圖逃脫罪責，而莎劇中的奧賽羅則是徒手掐死妻子並最終自刎身亡。這種人道主義的改寫，明顯降低了劇中人野蠻行徑的程度。

417. bluntly *(adv.)* 鈍地，直率地，遲鈍地

英文 He speaks bluntly, madam. He's more of a soldier than a scholar.

原句 *He speaks home, madam. You may relish him more in the soldier than in the scholar.*

中文 他說話很直爽，夫人，您把他當作一個軍人，不把他當作一個學者，就會好一些。

418. hot-tempered *(adj.)* 性急的，易怒的

英文 He's hot-tempered, and he might try to strike you with his sword.

原句 *Sir, he's rash and very sudden in choler, and haply may strike at you.*

中文 他的個性暴躁、易怒，也許會向你動武。

●track *076*

419. besides *(adv.)* 此外，而且，在其他方面；*(prep.)* 在……之外，除……之外

420. marriage *(n.)* 結婚，婚姻，結婚典禮

英文 Besides the good news, we are also celebrating his marriage.

原句 *For besides these beneficial news, it is the celebration of his nuptial.*

中文 除了這些好消息，同時還要祝賀將軍新婚。

---

421. announcement *(n.)* 通告，布告，宣告

英文 That's the end of the announcement.

原句 *So much was his pleasure should be proclaimed.*

中文 以上是將軍要公告週知的事。

第二幕
第三景

●track *077*

---

422. guard *(vt.)* 保衛，看守，監視；*(vi.)* 防範，守衛；
(n.) 衛兵，警戒，看守

英文 Good Michael, keep a careful eye on the guards tonight.

原句 *Good Michael, look you to the guard tonight.*

中文 好邁克爾，今晚請你留心戒備。

---

423. exquisitely *(adv.)* 精緻地，強烈地，光彩動人地

英文 She's an exquisitely beautiful lady.

原句 *She's a most exquisite lady.*

中文 她真的是一個絕代佳人。

---

424. twist up *(ph.)* 向上曲折盤旋，捲成螺旋形

425. toast *(vt.)* , *(vi.)* 舉杯祝酒；*(n.)* 祝酒，敬酒

英文 That fool Roderigo, all twisted up inside with love, has been drinking toasts to Desdemona by the gallon, and he's on guard duty

原句 *Now, my sick fool Roderigo, whom love hath turned almost the wrong side out, to Desdemona hath tonight caroused.*

中文 那位為情憔悴的傻瓜洛德里格，今晚敬了德絲苔蒙娜很多酒，他還要站崗守夜。

426. knock *(vt.)* , *(vi.)* 敲，擊，打，相撞；*(n.)* 敲，擊，打，挫折

英文 Let me go, or I'll knock you on the head.

原句 *Let me go, sir, or I'll knock you o'er the mazzard.*

中文 放開我，否則我要打你的頭。

427. savage *(adj.)* 野性的，野蠻的，原始的；*(n.)* 野蠻人，粗魯的人

英文 Have we all become as savage as the Turks, treating each other as badly as they would have treated us?

原句 *Are we turned Turks, and to ourselves do that which heaven hath forbid the Ottomites?*

中文 難道我們都變成像土耳其那樣的野蠻人，竟然自相殘殺起來？

428. in the world *(ph.)* (用於疑問詞) 到底，全世界

429. risk *(vt.)* 以……作為賭注，冒……的風險；*(n.)* 危險，風險

430. brawler *(n.)* 爭吵者，打架者

英文 What in the world made you risk your reputation like this and become a street brawler?

原句 *What's the matter, that you unlace your reputation thus and spend your rich opinion for the name of a night-brawler?*

中文 你到底為了什麼要犧牲寶貴的名譽，變成一個打架鬧事的街頭混混？

431. seriously *(adv.)* 嚴肅地，當真地，嚴重地

英文 I've been seriously hurt and your officer Iago can tell you what happened.

原句 *I am hurt to danger; your officer, Iago, can inform you.*

中文 我傷得很重，無法多說話，您的部下伊阿高可以告訴您發生什麼事。

432. diverge *(vt.)* 使分叉，使偏離；*(vi.)* 分叉，偏離，離題

英文 If you diverge from the truth in any way, you're not a true soldier.

原句 *If partially affined or leagued in office, thou dost deliver more or less than trut, thou art no soldier.*

中文 如果你存心偏袒，因而所說的話不符事實，你就不配是個軍人。

433. impose on *(ph.)* 強使某人接受……

英文 A reputation is a useless and fake quality that others impose on us.

原句 *Reputation is an idle and most false imposition, oft got without merit and lost without deserving.*

中文 比起能加諸於我們身上的其他事物，名譽是沒用、騙人的東西。

434. influence *(vt.)* 影響，感化； *(n.)* 影響，有影響的人（或事物）

英文 Our general's wife has a lot of influence now.

原句 *Our general's wife is now the general.*

中文 我們主帥的夫人對主帥有很大的影響力。

435. intelligence *(n.)* 智能，情報

英文 We achieve things with our intelligence, not by magic, and intelligent planning takes time.

原句 *Thou know'st we work by wit and not by witchcraft, and wit depends on dilatory time.*

中文 我們是依靠計謀達成目的，並非用魔法，既然用計謀就要等時機成熟。

第二幕
第一景

●track *078*

| **436.** | general *(adj.)* 普遍的，全體的；*(n.)* 將軍，上將 |

| **437.** | really *(adv.)* (用以加強語氣) 實在，實際上，十分 |

英文 But as they said, the general isn't really in the mood to hear music.

原句 *But, as they say, to hear music the general does not greatly care.*

中文 可是正像大家說的，將軍對音樂不大感興趣。

| **438.** | pack up *(ph.)* 不再做某事，放棄某事物 |

英文 Then pack up your pipes and go away.

原句 *Then put up your pipes in your bag, for I'll away.*

中文 那麼把你們的笛子收起來，然後離開吧！

| **439.** | under the circumstances *(ph.)* 在這樣的情況下 |

| **440.** | reproach *(vt.)* 責備，斥責；*(n.)* 責備，指摘 |

英文 The Moor says the man you hurt is very important in Cyprus, and that under the circumstances he has no choice but to reproach you.

原句 *The Moor replies that he you hurt is of great fame*

in Cyprus and great affinity, and that in wholesome
wisdom he might not but refuse you.

中文 將軍説，被你傷害的那個人，在賽普勒斯很有權勢，在那個情況下，他不得不斥責你。

● track *079*

---

441. look for (*ph.*) 尋找; 期待

英文 Look for me there when you come back.

原句 *Repair there to me.*

中文 你把事情辦好以後，到那邊和我會合。

---

442. at one's service (*ph.*) 聽候某人吩咐，隨時幫助某人

英文 We're at your service, my lord.

原句 *We'll wait upon your lordship.*

中文 我們願意奉陪，將軍。

● track *080*

---

443. political (*adj.*) 政治的，政黨的

---

444. consideration *(n.)* 考慮，動機，體貼，關心

英文 Those political considerations might last such a long time that the general will forget my love and service, especially if I'm gone and someone else has my job.

原句 *That policy may either last so long, or feed upon such nice and waterish diet, or breed itself so out of circumstance, that, I being absent and my place supplied, my general will forget my love and service.*

中文 這個權宜之計的時間可能會拖得很長，使得將軍忘記我對他的愛和忠誠，尤其萬一有人代替了我的職位。

---

445. witness *(vt.)* 目擊，為……作證；*(vi.)* 作證，證明；*(n.)* 目擊者，證據

豆知識
摩爾人的意義

　　文藝復興時期的摩爾是模糊、多樣、矛盾、富有爭議的。評論界認為「摩爾」一詞是深色膚色人的統稱，並可以與「非裔」、「衣索比亞人」、「黑人」、「印度人」等詞互換使用。在第三幕第三景中奧賽羅斥責德絲苔蒙娜的罪像「自己的臉一樣黑。」；她的膚色則與奧賽羅的膚色形成對比，在第五幕第二景中描述「她的皮膚比雪更白」。在伊麗莎白時期，「黑色」一詞的意義可能加入了廣義負面的暗示。

---

446. promise *(vt.)* 允諾，給人以⋯⋯的指望；*(vi.)* 允諾，作出保證，有前途；*(n.)* 承諾，希望，前途

---

447. position *(n.)* 位置，姿勢，職位

英文 Emilia here will be my witness: I promise you that you'll get your position back again.

原句 *Before Emilia here I give thee warrant of thy place.*

中文 當著愛蜜莉雅的面，我保證你一定可以回復原職。

---

448. petitioner *(n.)* 請求人，請願人

---

449. suffer from *(ph.)* 受⋯⋯困擾，受⋯⋯之苦

英文 I was talking to a petitioner here just now, someone who's suffering from your anger.

原句 *I have been talking with a suitor here, a man that languishes in your displeasure.*

中文 剛才有人在這兒向我請托，他因為失去了您的歡心，非常抑鬱不快。

---

450. mutter *(vt.)*, *(vi.)*, *(n.)* 低聲嘀咕，咕噥，抱怨

英文 I can't imagine you ask me for something and I tell you no or stand there muttering.

原句 *I wonder in my soul, what you would ask me that I should deny, or stand so mamm'ring on.*

中文 我想要是你有什麼事情要求我，我決不會拒絕你，或是如此地吞吞吐吐。

451. back and forth *(ph.)* 來來回回地

(英文) Oh, yes. He carried messages back and forth between us very often.

(原句) *Oh, yes, and went between us very oft.*

(中文) 啊，是的，他經常來往我們之間幫忙傳遞消息。

452. involve *(vt.)* 使捲入，使專注，使忙於

453. woo *(vt.)* 向⋯⋯求愛，追求；*(vi.)* 求愛，求婚，懇求

(英文) And when I told you he was involved the whole time I was trying to woo Desdemona, you were like, "Oh, really?"

(原句) *And when I told thee he was of my counsel of in my whole course of wooing, thou cried'st "Indeed?"*

(中文) 當我告訴你，我追求德絲苔蒙娜的全部過程中他都參與了，你又說「真的！」

454. frown *(vt.)* , *(vi.)* , *(n.)* 皺眉

455. wrinkle up *(ph.)* 使起皺紋

(英文) And then you frowned and wrinkled up your forehead as if you were imagining something horrible.

(原句) *And didst contract and purse thy brow together, as if thou then hadst shut up in thy brain some horrible conceit.*

(中文) 你蹙緊眉頭，好像是有可怕的想法在你的腦中。

456. victim *(n.)* 犧牲者，遇難者，受害者

457. devour *(vt.)* 狼吞虎嚥地吃，吞沒，毀滅

英文 Beware of jealousy, my lord! It's a green-eyed monster that makes fun of the victims it devours.

原句 *Oh, beware, my lord, of jealousy! It is the green-eyed monster which doth mock the meat it feeds on.*

中文 將軍，您要留心嫉妒啊！那是一個綠眼的妖魔，誰做了它的犧牲品，就要受它的玩弄。

458. the most *(ph.)* 某事的極限

英文 She lied to her father to marry you. And when she seemed to be afraid of you, she loved you the most.

原句 *She did deceive her father, marrying you; and when she seemed to shake and fear your looks, she loved them most.*

中文 她當初跟您結婚，曾經騙過她的父親；當她似乎對您感到畏懼時，她的心裡卻熱烈地愛著您。

459. destined *(adj.)* 命中注定的

英文 It's our destiny, like death. We are destined to be betrayed when we are born.

原句 *'Tis destiny unshunnable, like death: even then this forkèd plague is fated to us when we do quicken.*

中文 那就像死亡一樣是不可逃避的命運，我們一生下來就註定會被背叛。

460. handkerchief *(n.)* 手帕，紙巾，圍巾

461. keepsake *(n.)* 紀念品

英文 I'm glad I found this handkerchief. It's the first keepsake the Moor gave her.

原句 *I am glad I have found this napkin; this was her first remembrance from the Moor.*

中文 我很高興拾到了這條手帕；這是摩爾人裡第一次送她的紀念品。

462. absolute *(adj.)* 絕對的，確鑿的；*(n.)* 絕對事物

463. meaningless *(adj.)* 無意義的，無目的的

英文 To a jealous man, a meaningless little thing like air looks like an absolute proof.

原句 *Trifles light as air are to the jealous confirmations strong as proofs of holy writ.*

中文 對於一個嫉妒的人來說，像空氣一樣的小事，也會變成確切的證據。

464. suspicion *(vt.)* 懷疑，嫌疑；*(n.)* 懷疑

英文 It's a reason for suspicion, even though it's just a dream.

原句 *'Tis a shrewd doubt, though it be but a dream.*

中文 這樣就有理由懷疑這些事情，即使那只是一個夢。

●track *081*

465. on earth *(ph.)* 世界上，(常用於疑問句後加強語氣) 究竟，到底

英文 What on earth does that mean?

原句 *Can anything be made of this?*

中文 那究竟是什麼意思？

466. moist *(adj.)* 潮濕的，多雨的，含淚的

英文 Give me your hand. This hand is moist, my lady.

原句 *Give me your hand. Your hand's moist, my lady.*

中文 把你的手給我。妳的手很潮濕，我的夫人。

467. bother *(vt.)* 煩擾，使惱怒，使困惑； *(vi.)* 煩惱，費心； *(n.)* 煩惱，麻煩

英文 I have a bad cold that's bothering me. Lend me your handkerchief.

原句 *I have a salt and sorry rheum offends me. Lend me thy handkerchief.*

中文 我著涼流涕很難過，把妳的手帕借給我。

468. yell *(vt.)* , *(vi.)* , *(n.)* 叫喊，吼叫

英文 Why are you yelling at me so angrily?

原句 *Why do you speak so startingly and rash?*

中文 你為什麼說話這麼暴躁？

469. wedding day *(n.)* 結婚日，結婚紀念日

英文 We shouldn't expect men to be perfect, or for them to be as polite as on the wedding day.

原句 *Nay, we must think men are not gods, nor of them look for such observances as fit the bridal.*

中文 我們不能期待男人都很完美，也不能希望他們永遠會像新婚時那樣殷勤體貼。

---

470. monster *(n.)* 怪物，巨獸，兇惡的人

英文 They're never jealous for a reason; they're just jealous. It's like a monster that just grows and grows, out of nothing.

原句 *They are not ever jealous for the cause, but jealous for they're jealous; 'tis a monster begot upon itself, born on itself.*

中文 他們不會因為什麼理由而嫉妒，只是為了嫉妒而嫉妒，那是一個憑空而來、不斷生長的怪物。

第四幕第一景

● track *082*

---

471. as long as *(ph.)* 只要，既然

---

472. minor *(adj.)* 較小的，不重要的，次要的；*(n.)* 未成年人，副修科目

英文 As long as they didn't do anything, it would only be a minor sin.

(原句) *So they do nothing, 'tis a venial slip.*

(中文) 只要他們沒有做任何事，那這不過是一個小小的過失。

473. tremble *(vi.)*, *(n.)* 發抖，震顫

(英文) I wouldn't be trembling like this if I didn't know deep down this was all true.

(原句) *Nature would not invest herself in such shadowing passion without some instruction.*

(中文) 要不是深知這全部是真的，我也不會氣得發抖。

474. prostitute *(vt.)* 使賣淫；*(n.)* 娼妓

(英文) Now I'll ask Cassio about Bianca, a prostitute who sells her body for food and clothes.

(原句) *Now will I question Cassio of Bianca, A huswife that by selling her desires Buys herself bread and clothes.*

(中文) 現在我要向凱西歐談起碧安卡，一個靠著出賣風情維持生活的娼妓。

475. strangle *(vt.)* 勒死，絞死，使窒息；*(vi.)* 被絞死，窒息而死

476. contaminate *(vt.)* 弄髒，汙染，毒害

(英文) Strangle her in her bed, the same bed she's contaminated.

(原句) *Strangle her in her bed, even the bed she hath contaminated.*

(中文) 在床上勒死她，就在那被她玷污了的床上。

477. emotional *(adj.)* 感情的，易動情的

478. rattle *(vt.)* 使發出咯咯聲；*(vi.)* 發出咯咯聲，喋喋不休地講話；*(n.)* 響尾蛇尾端響環，喋喋不休

英文 Is this the guy who's supposed to never get emotional, and who never gets rattled, no matter what disaster happens?

原句 *Is this the nature whom passion could not shake? whose solid virtue the shot of accident nor dart of chance could neither graze nor pierce?*

中文 這就是那個不論遇到什麼磨難，喜怒之情不會形於外，而且不會驚惶失措的人嗎？

豆知識
奧賽羅的評價

　　對奧賽羅的評價因時代而有所不同。有的時代評論奧賽羅是「莎士比亞筆下最浪漫的主角」、「是其中最富詩意的人。」；有的認為他十分「任性」；也有人評價「這摩爾人的本性是高貴的，但他所流的血卻十分易燃、一點就爆。」。

第四幕
第一景

---

479. syllable *(n.)* 音節，(常用於否定句) 一言半語

英文 But I didn't see anything wrong, and I heard every syllable they said.

原句 *But then I saw no harm, and then I heard each syllable that breath made up between them.*

中文 可是我沒有看到什麼不妥的地方，而且我聽見他們交談時的每一個字。

---

480. whisper *(vt.)* 低語，耳語，私語；*(vi.)* 低語，私語；*(n.)* 耳語，私語，傳聞

英文 Didn't they ever whisper?

原句 *What, did they never whisper?*

中文 他們不會說悄悄話嗎？

---

481. beg *(vt.)* , *(vi.)* 乞討，請求

---

482. furious *(adj.)* 狂怒的，強烈的

英文 I'm begging you on my knees to tell me what your words mean. I can tell you're furious, but I don't understand what you're saying.

原句 *Upon my knee, what doth your speech import? I understand a fury in your words, but not the words.*

中文 我跪下來請你告訴我，這些話是什麼意思？我知道你在生氣，可是我聽不懂你說的話。

---

483. unfaithful *(adj.)* 不忠實的，不忠於職守的，有外遇的，(翻譯、版本) 不可靠的

英文 Heaven knows you're as unfaithful as hell.

原句 *Heaven truly knows that thou art false as hell.*

中文 上天知道妳像地獄一樣淫邪。

---

484. crook *(vt.)* 使彎曲，使成鉤形；*(vi.)* 彎曲，成鉤形；*(n.)* 彎曲的東西；鉤

英文 Moor is being tricked by some crook, some terrible villain, some rotten bastard.

原句 *The Moor's abus'd by some most villainous knave, some base notorious knave, some scurvy fellow.*

中文 這個摩爾人一定是上了不知哪個騙子的當，一個下流的混蛋，一個卑鄙的傢伙。

---

485. complaint *(n.)* 抱怨，抗議，怨言

英文 Your complaint against me is perfectly understandable, but I still insist I've done everything I could to help you.

原句 *Thou hast taken against me a most just exception, but yet I protest I have dealt most directly in thy affair.*

中文 你的責備都非常有理，可是我要說的是我所做的每一件事，都是為了幫助你。

第四幕
第二景

● track *084*

| 486. | displease *(vt.)* 使不高興，使討厭；*(vi.)* 使人不高興，使人生氣 |

英文 We shouldn't displease him.

原句 *We must not now displease him.*

中文 我們現在不能再惹他生氣。

| 487. | wrap *(vt.)* 包，裹，纏繞；*(vi.)* 纏繞，重疊；*(n.)* 包裹物，覆蓋物 |

| 488. | coffin *(n.)* 棺材，靈柩 |

英文 If I die before you, do make sure I'm wrapped in those sheets in my coffin.

原句 *If I do die before thee, prithee, shroud me in one of these same sheets.*

中文 如果我比妳先死，請妳就用這些被褥做我的殮衣。

| 489. | nightgown *(n.)* 女睡袍，男用長睡衫 |

英文 Should I get your nightgown?

原句 *Shall I go fetch your nightgown?*

中文 我要不要把您的睡衣拿來？

490. figure out *(ph.)* 計算出，想出，理解

英文 Then tell them to treat us well, or let them figure out that the bad things we do are just what we learned from them.

原句 *Then let them use us well, else let them know, the ills we do, their ills instruct us so.*

中文 要讓他們善待我們，否則就讓他們知道我們所做的壞事，都是向他們學習的。

●track *085*

491. cripple *(vt.)* 使成跛子，使殘廢；*(n.)* 跛子，殘廢的人

英文 I'll be crippled forever! Help! Murder! murder!

原句 *I am maimed for ever. Help, ho! Murder! Murder!*

中文 我要終身殘廢了！救命！殺人了！殺人了！

492. groan *(vt.)* 呻吟著說；*(vi.)* 呻吟；*(n.)* 呻吟聲，哼聲

英文 Two or three men are groaning

原句 *Two or three groan.*

中文 有兩三個人在呻吟。

493. bloody *(vt.)* 使流血；*(adj.)* 血汙的，流血的，
嗜殺的；*(adv.)* 很，非常

494. uproar *(n.)* 騷亂，吵鬧，喧囂

英文 I didn't mean to ignore you—it's just because of this bloody uproar.

原句 *These bloody accidents must excuse my manners, that so neglected you.*

中文 這些流血的慘劇，使我失禮忽視了您。

495. make sure *(ph.)* 查明，設法確保，確定

英文 Let's go make sure Cassio's wounds are properly dressed.

原句 *Let's go see poor Cassio dressed.*

中文 讓我們去看凱西歐，確實把他的傷口包紮好。

● track *086*

496. shed *(vt.)* 流出，脫落，使瀉去 *(vi.)* 流出，溢出，脫落

497. marble *(adj.)* 大理石的，似大理石的，冷酷無情的；*(n.)* 大理石，大理石雕刻品

英文 But I won't shed any of her blood or scar that beautiful skin, whiter than snow and smooth as the finest marble.

原句 *Yet I'll not shed her blood, nor scar that whiter skin of hers than snow, and smooth as monumental alabaster.*

中文 不過我不會讓她流血，或是毀傷她那比雪更白、比大理石更膩滑的肌膚。

498. extinguish *(vt.)* 撲滅，熄滅，使消失

英文 If I extinguish the candle, I can light it again if I regret it.

原句 *If I quench thee, thou flaming minister, I can again thy former light restore, should I repent me.*

中文 我熄滅蠟燭之後，如果改變心意，仍舊可以重新點亮

499. pause *(vi.)* , *(n.)* 中斷，暫停，猶豫

英文 While I'm doing this, I can't pause for a moment.

原句 *Being done, there is no pause.*

中文 我一旦做了，就無法停止。

500. manipulate *(vt.)* 操作，運用，操縱

英文 I was not easily made jealous, but once I was tricked and manipulated, I worked myself into a frenzy.

原句 *Of one not easily jealous, but being wrought, perplexed in the extreme.*

中文 我本來是不容易嫉妒的人，可是被煽動操弄後，便發狂喪失心智。

Part **2.**

四大喜劇

劇情簡介

《威尼斯商人》
(The Merchant of Venice)

年輕貌美的富家女子柏西亞 (Portia)，根據父親的遺囑，得到了金、銀、鉛三個盒子。其中一個盒子裡面裝著她的畫像，如果哪位先生選擇了正確的盒子，那麼她將會嫁給那個男人。於是，求婚者從四面八方前來……

一位名叫巴薩尼奧 (Bassanio) 的年輕人，他下定決心要贏得柏西亞。但是，要想達成這個願望，必須準備一筆不算少的費用。於是，他向富有的威尼斯商人安東尼歐 (Antonio) 求助，希望這位好友能借給他三千個硬幣。不巧，安東尼歐的錢都投入了海上的貨物，一時拿不出那麼多錢。不過，安東尼歐是位非常看重友情的基督徒，他下定決心要成全朋友的好事，因此便以自己的信用為擔保，去幫安東尼歐借債。

接著，放高利貸的夏洛克 (Shylock) 成了安東尼歐的債主。夏洛克是一個貪得無厭、一毛不拔的守財奴，由於安東尼歐貸款給人從不要利息，並幫助夏洛克的女兒

私奔，這使得他極度痛恨安東尼歐，於是懷恨在心的夏洛克便想乘這個機會報復。借貸時雙方約定以三個月為期，期限一到如果無法還清債務，債權人便可以在債務人身上割一磅肉作為處罰。結果，安東尼歐海上貨物的運送受阻，沒有辦法按時間還款。於是夏洛克要求法庭准許他根據契約上的約定，割下安東尼歐身上的一磅肉。

在法庭上，夏洛克認為契約一旦訂立就必須守約，誰也不能違背或改變，並堅持要按照約定割一磅肉。儘管夏洛克的要求非常過分，但在場的所有人都必須承認，在威尼斯誰也沒有權力變更既成的法律。事實上，夏洛克就是為了報復、洩憤才會想要得到安東尼歐的一塊肉，問他得到那一磅肉又能怎樣？他卻說：「拿來釣魚也好。」

到最後關頭，夏洛克還是放下了屠刀。讓他改變主意的，並不是誰的哀求，也不是良心發現，仍然是契約。因為當初安東尼歐和夏洛克簽訂契約時，只規定要割一磅肉，卻隻字未提因割肉而流出來的血。律師抓住這一項疏忽，要求夏洛克在割肉的時候，不能讓安東尼歐流下一滴鮮血，否則就是違約。如果違約，他就是故意殺人，他的產業，按照威尼斯的法律，就要充公。

事情圓滿解決之後，巴薩尼奧為了表達謝忱和敬意，在不得已的情況下把婚戒送給律師。巴薩尼奧等人回家後，與柏西亞欣喜重逢，但他又因婚戒的事而受到柏西亞的戲弄。直至柏西亞拿出戒指，才真相大白，原來法

庭上的律師就是她。就在這時，傳來一項好消息：安東
尼歐的商船已滿載而歸，平安抵港。

● track *087*

---

501. venture *(vt.)* 使冒險，以……作賭注，大膽提出；
(vi.) 冒險，大膽行事；*(n.)* 企業，冒險，投機活動

英文 Believe me, if I had such risky business ventures in other countries, I'd worry too.

原句 *Believe me, sir, had I such venture forth, the better part of my affections would be with my hopes abroad.*

中文 相信我，要是我也有這麼一筆買賣在海外，我一定也會很擔憂。

---

502. constantly *(adv.)* 不斷地，時常地

---

503. blade *(n.)* 刀身，刀片，葉片，葉片狀物

英文 I'd constantly be tossing blades of grass into the air to find out which way the wind was blowing.

原句 *I should be still plucking the grass to know where sits the wind; peering in maps for ports and piers and roads.*

中文 我一定會不斷拔草丟到空中觀測風向。

504. scare *(vt.)* 驚嚇，使恐懼；*(vi.)* 受驚；*(adj.)* 駭人的；*(n.)* 驚恐，驚嚇

505. wipe out *(ph.)* 消滅，徹底摧毀

英文 I'd get scared every time I blew on my soup to cool it, thinking of how a strong wind could wipe out my ships.

原句 *My wind cooling my broth, would blow me to an ague when I thought what harm a wind too great at sea might do.*

中文 我每次吹涼熱湯時，就會覺得害怕，想到海面上的強風會損壞我的船。

506. obvious *(adj.)* 明顯的，顯著的

507. cargo *(n.)* (船、飛機、車輛裝載的) 貨物

英文 It's obvious. Antonio is sad because he's so worried about his cargo.

原句 *I know Antonio is sad to think upon his merchandise.*

中文 很顯然地，安東尼歐是因為擔心他的貨物而憂慮。

508. financial *(adj.)* 財政的，金融的，金融界的

英文 Thankfully my financial situation is healthy. I don't have all of my money invested in one ship, or one part of the world.

原句 *I thank my fortune for it, my ventures are not in one bottom trusted, nor to one place.*

中文 幸好我的財務狀況還過得去，我沒有把所有的錢財都

投資在一艘船上，或某一個地方。

509. get together *(ph.)* 聚集，收集

510. available *(adj.)* 可獲得的，可買到的，有空的

英文 Let us know when you want to get together. We're available.

原句 *We'll make our leisures to attend on yours.*

中文 你什麼時候想要聚一聚，我們一定奉陪。

永恆的高利貸者形象

　　十六世紀初期，英國資本主義迅速發展。專制王朝實行了有利於工商業發展的政策，得到新興中產階級的支持，《威尼斯商人》就是在這樣的背景產生的。這是一部諷刺性的喜劇，其主題是歌頌仁愛、友誼和愛情，同時也反映出資本主義早期中產階級與高利貸者之間的矛盾，表現出作者對資本主義社會中金錢、法律和宗教等問題的人文主義思想。另外，該劇的一個重要文學成就，就是塑造了夏洛克這一唯利是圖、冷酷無情高利貸者的典型形象。

---

511. actually *(adv.)* 實際上，真的，竟然

英文 It would be better if you actually applied it to your life.

原句 *They would be better if well followed.*

中文 要是能夠確切去實行，那就更好了。

---

512. solemn *(adj.)* 嚴肅的，正式的，神聖的

英文 If he's so sad and solemn when he's young, I can only imagine he'll become a weeping philosopher when he grows old.

原句 *I fear he will prove the weeping philosopher when he grows old, being so full of unmannerly sadness in his youth.*

中文 假如他年紀輕輕就這麼愁眉苦臉，我能想像他年老會變成一個多愁常落淚的哲學家。

---

513. awful *(adj.)* 可怕的，使人敬畏的，極壞的；
(adv.) 極其

---

514. sober up *(ph.)* 使醒酒或清醒

英文 He's pretty awful in the morning when he's sobering up, and even worse in the afternoon when he's drunk.

原句 *Very vilely in the morning, when he is sober, and most vilely in the afternoon, when he is drunk.*

中文 他在早上清醒的時候，就已經相當糟糕了，一到下午喝醉了酒，更是壞透了。

515. suitor *(n.)* 求婚者，請願者，請求者

英文 The four suitors are looking for you so they can say goodbye, madam.

原句 *The four strangers seek for you, madam, to take their leave.*

中文 小姐，那四位追求者要來向您告別。

第●一●幕
第●二●景

●track *089*

516. lend *(vt.)* 把……借給，貸款；*(vi.)* 貸款

517. interest *(vt.)* 使發生興趣，引起……的關心；*(n.)* 關注，利益，利息

英文 I hate him because he's a Christian. But more than that, I hate him because he stupidly lends money without interest, which lowers the interest rates here in Venice.

原句 *I hate him for he is a Christian; but more for that in low simplicity he lends out money gratis and brings down the rate of usance here with us in Venice.*

中文 我不但討厭他是個基督徒，更厭惡他愚蠢地借錢給人不拿利息，把在威尼斯放債的利率壓低了。

518. upper hand *(ph.)* 優勢；支配

519. grudge *(vt.)*, *(n.)* 怨恨，妒忌

英文 If I can just get the upper hand of him once, I'll satisfy my old grudge against him.

原句 *If I can catch him once upon the hip, I will feed fat the ancient grudge I bear him.*

中文 只要讓我抓住他的把柄，一定要痛快地向他報這一段舊仇。

520. raise *(vt.)* 舉起，增加，籌款，養育，飼養；*(n.)* 加薪，提高，賭注加碼

521. ducat *(n.)* 硬幣，現金

英文 If I remember correctly, I can't raise the entire three thousand ducats immediately.

原句 *And by the near guess of my memory I cannot instantly raise up the gross of full three thousand ducats.*

中文 假如我記得沒錯，我無法立刻湊足三千硬幣。

522. quote *(vt.)* 引用，引述；*(vi.)* 引用，引證；*(n.)* 引語，引文，引號

英文 The devil can quote Scripture for his own use.

原句 *The devil can cite Scripture for his purpose.*

中文 魔鬼也會引證《聖經》來替自己辯護。

---

523. embarrass *(vt.)* 使窘迫，使侷促不安，使困惑

---

524. humiliate *(vt.)* 使蒙恥辱，使丟臉

英文 I want to be friends with you, and forget all the times you've embarrassed and humiliated me.

原句 *I would be friends with you and have your love, forget the shames that you have stained me with.*

中文 我願意跟您交個朋友，得到您的友情；您從前加在我身上的種種羞辱，我願意完全忘掉。

---

525. repay *(vt.)* , *(vi.)* 償還，報答，報復

---

526. penalty *(n.)* 處罰，刑罰，罰款

英文 If you don't repay me on the day we agree on, in the place we name, for the sum of money fixed in our contract, your penalty will be a pound of your pretty flesh, to be cut off and taken out of whatever part of your body I like.

原句 *If you don't repay me on the day we agree on, in the place we name, for the sum of money fixed in our contract, your penalty will be a pound of your pretty flesh, to be cut off and taken out of whatever part of your body I like.*

中文 如果你沒有如期歸還我們在合約上寫明的全數借款，我會依照我的喜好隨意從你身上割下一磅的肉作為償款。

527. take chances (*ph.*) 冒險

英文 You have to take your chances.

原句 *You must take your chance.*

中文 你必須試試運氣。

528. beforehand (*adj.*) 預先準備好的，提前的；(*adv.*) 預先地，提前地

529. incorrectly (*adv.*) 錯誤地

英文 Either don't choose at all, or swear beforehand that if you choose incorrectly you'll never talk about marriage to any woman again.

原句 *And either not attempt to choose at all, or swear before you choose, if you choose wrong, never to speak to lady afterward in way of marriage.*

中文 你要嘛根本就別參與抽彩 (此指劇中的選親活動)，要嘛在選擇前事先發誓，萬一抽錯了，從此不再向任何女子求婚。

●track *091*

---

530. recognize *(vt.)* 認出，認識，認定；*(vi.)* 承認，確認

英文 Don't you recognize me, father?

原句 *Do you know me, Father?*

中文 您不認識我了嗎，父親？

---

531. wise *(adv.)* 有智慧的，聰明的，明智的

英文 It is a wise father who knows his own child.

原句 *It is a wise father that knows his own child.*

中文 聰明的父親才會認識自己的兒子。

---

532. come to light *(ph.)* 暴露，真相大白

英文 The truth will come to light, and murder can't be hidden long.

原句 *Truth will come to light; murder cannot be hid long.*

中文 事情會真相大白，殺人的兇手不可能躲藏太久。

---

533. flesh and blood *(ph.)* 血肉之軀，親人

英文 If you are Launcelot, then you are my own flesh and blood.

原句 *If thou be Launcelot, thou art mine own flesh and blood.*

中文 倘若你真的是朗斯洛特，那麼你就是我親骨肉。

534. starve *(vt.)* 使餓死，使挨餓，使急需；*(vi.)* 餓死，
挨餓，渴望

英文 He's starving me to death.

原句 *I am famished in his service.*

中文 我快被他餓死了。

● track *092*

535. cheer up *(ph.)* 高興起來

英文 It's hell in our house, and you helped cheer it up, like a funny devil.

原句 *Our house is hell, and thou, a merry devil, didst rob it of some taste of tediousness.*

中文 我們家是一座地獄，幸虧有你這淘氣鬼，讓氣氛歡樂許多。

536. heinous *(adj.)* 可憎的，兇惡的

英文 Oh God, what a heinous sinner I am, being ashamed to be my father's child!

原句 *Alack, what heinous sin is it in me to be ashamed to be my father's child!*

中文 老天，我真是罪惡深重，竟會羞於做我父親的孩子。

537. torchbearer *(n.)* 持火炬者

英文 We haven't even talked about who'll be our torchbearers.

原句 *We have not spoke us yet of torchbearers.*

中文 我們還沒有說好誰要拿火炬。

538. fail *(vt.)* , *(vi.)* 失敗，不及格；*(n.)* 不及格

英文 Tell Jessica I won't fail her.

原句 *Tell gentle Jessica I will not fail her.*

中文 告訴潔西卡我不會辜負她。

539. expect *(vt.)* 預期，期待，等待；*(vi.)* 期待，預期，懷孕

英文 My young master is expecting you.

原句 *My young master doth expect your reproach.*

中文 我們家少爺在等你。

540. masquerade *(vi.)* 參加化裝舞會，化裝，冒充；
(n.) 化裝舞會，偽裝

英文 What, there's going to be a masquerade?

原句 *What, are there masques?*

中文 什麼！要舉行化妝舞會嗎？

541. nasty *(adj.)* 令人作嘔的，卑鄙的，討厭的；
(n.) 討厭的人

金錢價值觀的對比

　　在《威尼斯商人》中，安東尼歐與夏洛克的對抗戰是商業資本與高利貸資本的對抗，也是新興中產階級人文主義和高利貸者極端利己主義信條的對抗。正如劇中柏西亞的求婚者在金、銀、鉛盒子中的選擇，實際上正是價值觀念的選擇，安東尼歐與夏洛克的對抗從另一個角度看也是道德衝突，展示的是對善與惡的不同理解，闡釋的是如何做人，如何待人。

542. squeal *(vt.)* , *(vi.)* 發出長而尖的聲音

英文 Listen to me, Jessica, lock my doors up, and when you hear the drum and the nasty squealing of the flute, don't climb up to the windows.

原句 *Hear you me, Jessica: lock up my doors; and when you hear the drum, and the vile squealing of the wry-necked fife, clamber not you up to the casements then.*

中文 聽好，潔西卡，把我的門鎖好。當妳聽見鼓聲和又長又尖銳的刺耳笛聲，不許爬到窗戶上張望。

第二幕
第六景

● track *095*

543. chase *(vt.)* , *(vi.)* , *(n.)* 追逐，追尋，追求

英文 We chase everything in life more excitedly than we actually enjoy it when we get it.

原句 *All things that are, Are with more spirit chasèd than enjoyed.*

中文 世間的任何事物，追求時的興致總要比享用時還要濃烈。

544. worth one's while *(ph.)* 值得某人花時間 (或精力) 的

英文 It'll be worth your while.

原句 *It is worth the pains.*

中文 這值得你這麼做。

545. each other *(ph.)* 彼此，互相

546. dress up *(ph.)* 盛裝，裝扮

英文 But love is blind, and lovers can't see the silly things they do around each other. If they could, Cupid himself would be embarrassed to see me dressed up as a boy.

原句 *But love is blind, and lovers cannot see the pretty follies that themselves commit; for if they could Cupid himself would blush to see me thus transformèd to a boy.*

中文 不過戀愛是盲目的，戀人們看不見他們自己所做的傻事；要是他們看得見的話，那麼丘比特看到我打扮成男孩子，也要感到臉紅。

第二幕
第七景

● track *096*

547. inscription *(n.)* 銘刻，碑文，題詞

英文 I'll look over the inscriptions again.

原句 *I will survey th' inscriptions back again.*

中文 我先把上面刻印的字再仔細看一遍。

548. in terms of *(ph.)* 就……方面來說

549. upbringing *(n.)* 養育，教養，培養

英文 By birth I deserve her. In terms of wealth, talents, and upbringing, and especially love, I deserve her.

原句 *I do in birth deserve her, and in fortunes, in graces, and in qualities of breeding; but more than these, in love I do deserve.*

中文 我和她門當戶對，不論是財產、才情、教養各方面，尤其是對她的深情，我都配得上她。

550. glitter *(vi.)* , *(n.)* 閃閃發光，閃爍，光彩

英文 All that glitters is not gold.

原句 *All that glitters is not gold.*

中文 會閃光的不全都是黃金。

●track *097*

551. concentrate *(vt.)* 集中，濃縮；*(vi.)* 集中，全神貫注；*(n.)* 濃縮物

英文 Be happy and concentrate your thoughts on love and how to win your love.

原句 *Be merry, and employ your chiefest thoughts to court-ship and such fair ostents of love as shall conveniently become you there.*

中文 你只管高高興興，全心全意去追求愛情、去贏得美人芳心。

---

552. loan *(vt.)*, *(vi.)* 借出； *(n.)* 借出，貸款

英文 I hope Antonio repays his loan on time, or he'll suffer for this.

原句 *Let good Antonio look he keep his day, or he shall pay for this.*

中文 我希望安東尼歐準時還了那筆債款，否則他就會遭殃。

● track *098*

---

553. oath *(n.)* 誓言，宣誓，詛咒

英文 The prince of Arragon has taken his oath, and he's coming to make his choice now.

原句 *The Prince of Arragon hath ta'en his oath and comes to his election presently.*

中文 阿拉岡親王已經宣誓過，接著要來抽彩了。

---

554. gamble *(vt.)*, *(vi.)*, *(n.)* 賭博，打賭，冒險

英文 Everyone who comes to gamble on winning me has to swear to these three rules.

原句 *To these injunctions every one doth swear that comes*

to hazard for my worthless self.

中文 每個想抽彩贏得婚事的人,都要發誓願意遵守這三個規定。

---

555. jump on *(ph.)* 跳上,責罵,批評

---

556. bandwagon *(ph.)* 遊行隊伍前的樂隊車,浪潮,時尚

---

557. crude *(adj.)* 天然的,未經加工的,沒教養的

英文 So I won't choose what many men desire, because I won't jump on the bandwagon and include myself with the whole crude population.

原句 *I will not choose what many men desire, because I will not jump with common spirits and rank me with the barbarous multitudes.*

中文 我不願選擇眾人追求的事物,因為我不要隨波逐流,也跟著成為庸俗的群眾。

---

558. moth *(n.)* 蛾,蠹,蛀蟲

---

559. flame *(vt.)* 點燃,激起,照亮; *(vi.)* 燃燒,臉泛紅; *(n.)* 火焰,熱情

英文 These men are like moths, drawn to these boxes as if they were flames.

原句 *Thus hath the candle singed the moth.*

中文 這些男人像是飛蛾,抽彩則仿如火光,吸引他們撲火。

---

560. likeable *(adj.)* 討人喜歡的

英文 I haven't seen such a likeable ambassador for your love.

原句 *Yet I have not seen so likely an ambassador of love.*

中文 我從來沒有見過這麼一位討人喜歡的愛神使者。

---

561. gossip *(vi.)*, *(n.)* 閒聊，流言蜚語

---

562. claim *(vt.)* 提出要求，聲稱，主張；*(vi.)*，
(n.) 提出要求

英文 I hope this new rumor is a lie, like the gossiping widow's claim that she was sorry her third husband died!

原句 *I would she were as lying a gossip in that as ever knapped ginger, or made her neighbors believe she wept for the death of a third husband.*

中文 我希望那些謠傳跟愛嚼舌根的寡婦所扯說的謊一樣，說她為第三任丈夫的死難過，根本是靠不住的鬼話。

---

563. outdo *(vt.)* 勝過，超越

英文 I'll treat you as badly as you taught me to, and you'll be lucky if I don't outdo my teachers.

原句 *The villainy you teach me I will execute, and it shall go hard but I will better the instruction.*

中文 我一定會依照著你們教給我的惡行對待你們，而且還要變本加厲。

| **564.** | a number of *(ph.)* 一些 |

| **565.** | creditor *(n.)* 債權人；貸方 |

| **566.** | go bankrupt *(ph.)* 破產 |

英文 I came to Venice with a number of Antonio's creditors who say he won't be able to avoid going bankrupt.

原句 *There came divers of Antonio's creditors in my company to Venice that swear he cannot choose but break.*

中文 有幾個跟我同路到威尼斯的安東尼歐債主，他們說他這次一定會破產。

這是「人」的勝利

　　《威尼斯商人》一劇的主角安東尼歐是一個心腸仁慈的人、多情尚義的人，在他身上存留著比任何義大利人更多的古羅馬俠義猜神，安東尼歐人格的高尚，是莎士比亞對人的肯定與對人的高尚品質的頌揚。因此，安東尼歐的最後勝利是「人」的勝利，是人文主義的勝利。夏洛克的敗訴，是反人文主義者的失敗。莎士比亞在安東尼歐與夏洛克的對抗中，不僅凝聚生動的戲劇性和濃濃的喜劇色彩，更成功地高揚起人文主義的旗幟。

567. hound *(vt.)* 追獵，追逼，催促；*(n.)* 獵犬

英文 I'll hound him. I'll torture him. I'm very glad.

原句 *I'll plague him. I'll torture him. I am glad of it.*

中文 我要逼迫他，我要讓他受罪。這樣做讓我感到高興。

568. in exchange for *(ph.)* 作為……的交換

英文 One creditor showed me a ring he got from your daughter in exchange for a monkey.

原句 *One of them showed me a ring that he had of your daughter for a monkey.*

中文 有一個債權人給我看一隻戒指，說你女兒拿它跟他交換一隻猴子。

●track *100*

569. bewitch *(vt.)* 施魔術於，使陶醉，使銷魂

英文 God, your eyes have bewitched me. They've divided me in two.

原句 *Beshrew your eyes, they have o'erlooked me and divided me.*

中文 老天，你的眼睛迷惑了我，把我分成兩半。

570. confess a crime *(ph.)* 認罪

571. treason (*n.*) 叛國罪，謀反罪，背叛

英文 Then confess to your crime. Tell us about the treason you've mixed in with your love.

原句 *Then confess what treason there is mingled with your love.*

中文 那麼向我招認，你的愛情中隱藏著什麼樣的背叛？

572. daybreak (*n.*) 黎明，破曉

573. bridegroom (*n.*) 新郎

英文 It's the sweet sounds at daybreak that the dreaming bridegroom hears on his wedding morning, calling him to the church.

原句 *Such it is as are those dulcet sounds in break of day that creep into the dreaming bridegroom's ear, and summon him to marriage.*

中文 那是黎明時分穿進正在做著好夢的新郎耳中，催促他去婚禮教堂的甜蜜樂音。

574. appearance (*n.*) 出現，外貌，外觀

英文 You can't always judge a book by its cover. People are often tricked by false appearances.

原句 *So may the outward shows be least themselves. The world is still deceived with ornament.*

中文 事物的外觀和本質經常不相符合，世人也往往會為外表欺騙。

575. manage to *(ph.)* 成功的完成，設法

英文 Every sin in the world manages to make itself look good somehow.

原句 *There is no vice so simple but assumes some mark of virtue on his outward parts.*

中文 任何罪惡都可以在表象上裝出有美德的樣子。

576. depend on *(ph.)* 視某事物而定，依靠，信賴

英文 Your fate depended on those boxes, and it turns out that mine did too.

原句 *Your fortune stood upon the casket there, and so did mine too, as the matter falls.*

中文 你的命運靠那幾個盒子來決定，結果我的命運也是。

577. bear *(vt.)* 支持，承擔 *(n.)* 熊

578. burden *(vt.)* 加重壓於，加負擔於；*(n.)* 重擔，負擔

英文 I'm half of you, so let me bear half the burden this letter brings you.

原句 *I am half yourself, and I must freely have the half of anything that this same paper brings you.*

中文 我是你的另一半，不論這封信所帶給你什麼不幸的消息，也讓我分擔一半。

579. certainly *(adv.)* 無疑地，確實，沒問題

580. collateral *(adj.)* 附屬的；*(n.)* 擔保品，抵押品

---

581. debt *(n.)* 債，借款

英文 I couldn't pay my debt to the Jew on the due date. Since I'll certainly die when he takes his collateral out of my flesh, all debts are cleared between you and me if I can just see you again before I die

原句 *And since in paying it, it is impossible I should live, all debts are cleared between you and I, if I might but see you at my death.*

中文 我無法如期清償債務，因此依約我要割身上的肉償還。看來我是活不了，那麼只要你在我死前見一面，我們之間的債就算還清了。

第三幕
第三景

● track *101*

---

582. jailer *(n.)* 監獄看守，獄卒

---

583. convince *(vt.)* 使確信，使信服，說服

英文 Jailer, watch out for this one. Don't try to convince me to feel sorry for him.

原句 *Jailer, look to him. Tell not me of mercy.*

中文 獄官，好好看住他，別想說服我同情他。

---

584. that's why... *(ph.)* 那是⋯⋯的原因

英文 I've often given money to people who were unable to pay back their loans to him. That's why he hates me.

原句 *I oft delivered from his forfeitures. Many that have at times made moan to me. Therefore he hates me.*

中文 有時候他逼人還債，他們情急之下向我求救，我經常幫忙他們，因此他才會恨我。

● track *102*

585.	take charge of *(ph.)* 管理，負責

586.	management *(n.)* 管理，經營，處理

英文 I have a favor to ask of you. Lorenzo, please take charge of the management of my house until my husband comes back.

原句 *Lorenzo, I commit into your hands the husbandry and manage of my house until my lord's return.*

中文 羅蘭佐，我要請你在我的丈夫回來以前，幫忙照管我家。

587.	immature *(adj.)* 未成熟的，未臻完美的

英文 I know a thousand immature tricks like that, and I'll use them all.

原句 *I have within my mind a thousand raw tricks of these* *bragging jacks, which I will practice.*

中文 這種淘氣把戲我腦中多很，都可以拿出來用。

●track *103*

588. straightforward *(adj.)* , *(adv.)* 一直向前，直截了當

英文 I've always been straightforward with you, so now I'm telling you what I think.

原句 *I was always plain with you, and so now I speak my agitation of the matter.*

中文 我一向喜歡對你說實話，所以現在我也把心中想的告訴你。

589. pun *(n.)* 雙關語，俏皮話

590. parrot *(vt.)* 重複地說話；*(n.)* 鸚鵡

英文 Any fool can make puns! I think the most articulate person will soon be silence, and talking will only be a good thing for parrots to do.

原句 *How every fool can play upon the word! I think the best grace of wit will shortly turn into silence, and discourse grow commendable in none only but parrots.*

中文 連傻瓜都能說起俏皮話來！我想很快連口才最好的人，都要默不作聲了，到時候就只剩下鸚鵡敢開口說話。

591. ruthless *(adj.)* 無情的，殘忍的

592. inhuman *(adj.)* 無人性的，野蠻的，硬心腸的

593. incapable *(adj.)* 不能勝任的，無能的

英文 You've come to face a ruthless enemy, an inhuman wretch incapable of pity, without any feelings of mercy.

原句 *Thou art come to answer a stony adversary, an inhuman wretch uncapable of pity, void and empty from any dram of mercy.*

中文 你遇到一個鐵石心腸的對手，他是個殘酷、毫無同情心的壞蛋。

594. decay *(vt.)* 使腐朽，使腐爛，使牙齒蛀壞；*(vi.)*，*(n.)* 腐朽，腐爛，衰敗

英文 You're going to ask me why I'd rather have a pound of decaying flesh than three thousand ducats.

原句 *You'll ask me why I rather choose to have a weight of carrion flesh than to receive three thousand ducats.*

中文 你一定會問我為什麼不願接受三千硬幣，而寧願拿一塊會腐爛的肉。

595. exterminate *(vt.)* 根除，滅絕，消滅

英文 What if I had a rat in my house, and I felt like paying ten thousand ducats to have it exterminated?

原句 *What if my house be troubled with a rat, and I be pleased to give ten thousand ducats to have it baned?*

中文 要是我的屋子裏有老鼠，我高興花一萬個硬幣消除它，誰管得了我？

596. excuse *(vt.)* 原諒，辯解，成為……的理由；
(n.) 原諒，辯解，藉口

英文 That's no answer, you heartless man. It doesn't excuse your cruel behavior.

原句 *This is no answer, thou unfeeling man, to excuse the current of thy cruelty.*

中文 你這冷酷無情的人，這樣的回答無法替你的殘忍行為辯解。

597. expensive *(adj.)* 昂貴的，花錢的

英文 The pound of flesh that I want from him was very expensive.

原句 *The pound of flesh which I demand of him is dearly bought.*

中文 我向他要求的這一磅肉，是我付高價買的。

598. knife *(n.)* 刀，小刀，匕首

599. sole *(vt.)* 換鞋底；*(adj.)* 僅有的；*(n.)* 腳底，鞋底

英文 You're sharpening that knife not on your sole but on your soul, you cruel Jew.

原句 *Not on thy sole, but on thy soul, harsh Jew, thou makest thy knife keen.*

中文 狠心的猶太人，你不是在鞋底磨刀，而是在你的靈魂上磨刀。

600. taunt *(vt.)* , *(n.)* 辱罵，嘲笑，奚落

601. wear out *(ph.)* 用壞，穿破，耗盡

英文 Unless your taunts can undo the signature on my contract, you're just wearing out your lungs by speaking so loud.

原句 *Till thou canst rail the seal from off my bond, thou but offend'st thy lungs to speak so loud.*

中文 除非你的辱罵能夠毀掉契約上的簽章，否則像你這樣大聲謾罵只是傷肺而已。

602. well-educated *(adj.)* 有教養的

英文 This letter from Bellario introduces us to a young and well-educated legal expert.

原句 *This letter from Bellario doth commend a young and learnèd doctor to our court.*

中文 培拉里歐在這封信上引薦了一位年輕有學問的法律專家。

603. consult *(vt.)* 與……商量，看病，查閱；*(vi.)* 商議，當顧問

英文 We consulted many books together.

原句 *We turned o'er many books together.*

中文 我們一起查閱很多書。

604. take responsibility for *(ph.)* 承擔責任

英文 I take all responsibility for my decisions.

原句 *My deeds upon my head.*

中文 我自己做的事，我自己承擔！

---

605. malicious *(adj.)* 惡意的，懷恨的

英文 If that's not enough, then you're just evil and malicious.

原句 *If this will not suffice, it must appear that malice bears down truth.*

中文 要是這樣還不能滿足你，那你就是存心害人。

---

606. establish *(vt.)* 建立，設立，創辦

---

607. decree *(vt.)* , *(vi.)* 頒布，命令，注定；*(n.)* 法令，命令，判決

英文 There's no power in Venice that can change an established decree.

原句 *There is no power in Venice can alter a decree established.*

中文 在威尼斯沒有人有權利改變既訂的法令。

---

608. more or less *(ph.)* 差不多，多少有一點

---

609. fraction *(n.)* 小部分，碎片，一點兒

---

610. confiscate *(adj.)* 被沒收的；*(vt.)* 沒收，將……充公

英文 If you take than exactly a pound, even if it's just the tiniest fraction of an ounce—if the scale changes by even so much as a hair, you will die, and all your property will be confiscated too.

原句 *If thou takest more or less than a just pound, be it but so much as makes it light or heavy in the* *substance, or the division of the twentieth part of one poor scruple, nay, if the scale do turn but in the estimation of a hair, thou diest and all thy goods are confiscate.*

中文 如果你割下來的肉，比一磅略微輕或重一點，即使相差只有一絲一毫，或者僅僅一根毫毛之微，就要處死刑，你的財產也要全部充公。

夏洛克的悲劇性

　　莎士比亞身處的時代圍繞著對猶太民族充滿敵視與偏見的社會環境，但他並沒有把《威尼斯商人》中的夏洛克寫成純粹邪惡的化身，而是在譴責夏洛克復仇的同時，也描寫了夏洛克所遭受的歧視，揭示出夏洛克惡的背後所包含的怨和恨，用現實主義的描述手法間接地揭示出造成人物衝突的宗教根源，使這齣喜劇暗含了深刻的悲劇性。

●track 105

611. accept *(vt.)* , *(vi.)* 接受，答應

英文 Please tell him I accept his ring with thanks.

原句 *His ring I do accept most thankfully.*

中文 他的戒指我收下了，請幫我謝謝他。

612. bet (that) *(ph.)* 敢斷定，確信

英文 I bet you'll be able to.

原句 *Thou mayst, I warrant.*

中文 我確信你一定能夠做到。

● track *106*

613. footstep *(n.)* 腳步,腳步聲,階梯

英文 I hear his footsteps

原句 *I hear the footing of a man.*

中文 我聽見腳步聲。

614. holler *(vt.)* , *(vi.)* , *(n.)* 叫喊

英文 Stop hollering, man! He's here.

原句 *Leave holloaing, man. Here.*

中文 別嚷啦,朋友,他就在這兒。

615. let the music fill⋯ *(ph.)* 讓音樂充滿⋯⋯

英文 Let's sit here and let the music fill our ears.

原句 *Here will we sit and let the sounds of music creep in our ears.*

中文 讓我們在這坐下來聆聽音樂。

616. stillness *(n.)* 靜止,寂靜

617. be perfect for *(ph.)* 對⋯⋯最適當的

英文 Stillness and nighttime are perfect for beautiful music.

原句 *Soft stillness and the night become the touches of sweet harmony.*

中文 靜寂的夜晚時刻,最適合欣賞美妙的音樂。

618. dim *(vt.)* 使變暗; *(vi.)* 變暗; *(n.)* 微暗的,暗淡的

Well, brighter lights always dim the smaller ones.

(原句) *So doth the greater glory dim the less.*

(中文) 比較暗的光會被比較亮的光遮掩。

---

619. as well as *(ph.)* 也，還，而且

---

620. lark *(n.)* 雲雀

---

621. nightingale *(n.)* 夜鶯

---

622. honk *(vt.)* 按喇叭表示；*(vi.)* 雁鳴，按汽車喇叭；
(n.) 雁鳴，汽車喇叭聲

 The crow sings as well as the lark when no one's listening. If the nightingale sang during the day, when every goose is honking, nobody would think it sang any better than a wren.

(原句) *The crow doth sing as sweetly as the lark when neither is attended, and I think the nightingale, if she should sing by day when every goose is cackling, would be thought no better a musician than the wren.*

(中文) 烏鴉的歌聲若沒有人欣賞，也就和雲雀一樣；如果夜鶯白天在聒噪的群鵝中歌唱，歌聲絕不會比鷦鷯更美。

---

623. cut short *(ph.)* 縮短，打斷

 But action speaks louder than words, so I'll cut short these polite words.

(原句) *It must appear in other ways than words, therefore I scant this breathing courtesy.*

中文 不過嘴上的空言無法表達誠意，所以我就不多說客套話了。

---

624. dishonor *(vt.)* 使丟臉，使受恥辱；*(n.)* 不名譽，丟臉

---

625. ungrateful *(adj.)* 忘恩負義的，不感激的，不領情的

英文 I just couldn't dishonor myself by acting ungrateful to him.

原句 *My honor would not let ingratitude so much besmear it.*

中文 我不能因為忘恩負義而讓我的名譽受損。

《仲夏夜之夢》
(A Midsummer Night's Dream)

　　根據古希臘時代的法律，父母有權力為女兒挑選結婚對象，如果女兒不接受安排，父母就有權利處死她。

　　雅典有兩個青年賴桑德 (Lysander) 和德米崔斯 (Demetrius) 同時愛上了美麗的荷米雅 (Hermia)，但荷米雅與賴桑德是一對戀人，她的好友海倫娜 (Helena) 則戀著德米崔斯。不過麻煩的是，荷米雅的父親反對他們在一起，更要求公爵下令，如果荷米雅不肯嫁給德米崔斯，就要判她死罪。荷米雅深愛賴桑德，又因德米崔斯曾對摯友海倫娜 (Helena) 示愛，所以不願意聽從父親的命令。於是，荷米雅和賴桑德決定私奔，並約好要在森林裡會合，海倫娜便將這消息告訴熱愛荷米雅和德米崔斯，兩人也跟隨這對戀人逃進森林，不料四個人一起迷失於森林中。

　　這個森林裡本來住著仙王奧伯龍 (Oberon)、仙后泰妲妮亞 (Titania) 和侍奉他們的小仙子、小精靈，此時仙王、仙后正為爭奪一個人類伺童而不和。仙王爭不過仙

后，為了讓仙后讓步，便派小精靈派克 (Puck) 去取來神奇紫花的汁液戲弄仙后。這種花因為被丘比特的箭射傷過，所以有一種魔力：如果將這汁液滴在睡眠中者的眼皮上，無論男女，醒來都會瘋狂地愛上第一眼看見的生物，不論是牛、馬、豬都會愛上。

仙王利用神奇的汁液使得仙后愛上一名戴著驢頭的工人。另一方面，仙王因同情海倫娜，就命令派克趁德米崔斯睡著時，把神奇的紫花汁液滴在他的眼臉上，等到他醒來，就會愛上睜開眼後第一個看到的人。不料陰錯陽差，派克搞錯對象，把汁液滴在賴桑德的眼上，使賴桑德愛上海倫娜。賴桑德醒來時一眼看見誤闖進來的海倫娜，因而「移情別戀」對海倫娜大獻殷勤，這讓可憐的荷米雅傷心萬分；而德米崔斯醒來時第一眼看見的恰是被精靈引來的海倫娜，因而愛瘋狂愛上她，這讓海倫娜苦惱萬分，以為他們三個人有意聯合起來取笑她。最後，賴桑德和德米崔斯甚至為了爭取海倫娜的愛而準備決鬥。

四人因為派克的淘氣捉弄而爭吵不休，隨後因體力不支而昏睡在森林中，仙王便命令派克趁此時趕緊把紫花汁液滴在賴桑德的眼裡，這次他醒來看到的是荷米雅，他覺得之前對荷米雅的愛轉移給海倫娜，好像人在感冒時會改變胃口，本來愛吃的食物都變得不愛了，等感冒好了，胃口又恢復了。荷米雅的父親發現荷米雅和德米崔斯各有意中人後，也就不再堅持自己的安排，最後就

答應了荷米雅和賴桑德的婚事，讓這兩對戀人雙雙在同一天舉行婚禮。而仙王也得到侍童，解除對仙后所施的魔力，精靈們又回復到以往的快樂，兩對情侶也從此過著幸福快樂的日子。

●track *107*

---

626. fade away *(ph.)* 漸弱，死亡

---

627. stepson *(n.)* 繼子

---

628. inheritance *(n.)* 繼承，遺產，傳統

英文 The old moon is taking too long to fade away to keep me from getting what I want, just like an old widow makes her stepson wait to get his inheritance.

原句 *But oh, methinks how slow this old moon wanes! She lingers my desires, like to a stepdame or a dowager long withering out a young man's revenue.*

中文 這個下弦月消逝得多麼慢，延誤了我的期待，就像是一個老寡婦，故意拖延著要給繼子的遺產。

---

629. melancholy *(adj.)* 憂鬱的；*(n.)* 憂鬱

---

630. funeral *(adj.)* 喪葬的；*(n.)* 喪葬，葬儀

英文 Melancholy is only appropriate for funerals. We don't want it at our festivities.

原句 *Turn melancholy forth to funerals; the pale companion is not for our pomp.*

中文 憂愁只適合葬禮，不要出現在我們的婚禮上。

---

631. token *(adj.)* 作為標記的；象徵性的；*(n.)* 標記，象徵，紀念品

英文 You, you, Lysander, you've written poems for my daughter, and exchanged tokens of love with her.

原句 *Thou, thou, Lysander, thou hast given her rhymes; and interchanged love tokens with my child.*

中文 你，你，賴桑德，你寫詩給我女兒，和她交換愛情的信物。

---

632. priestess *(n.)* 女祭司，女神職人員

---

633. stem *(vt.)* 抽去……的梗；*(vi.)* 起源於；*(n.)* 莖，樹幹，葉柄，血統

英文 A married woman is like a rose who is picked and made into a beautiful perfume, while a priestess just withers away on the stem.

原句 *But earthlier happy is the rose distilled, than that which withering on the virgin thorn grows, lives, and dies in single blessedness.*

中文 結婚的女子有如被摘下提煉的玫瑰，製成了誘人的香水，而終身未嫁的女祭司則如長在樹枝上的花，終將

要凋萎落地。

| **634.** | obstacle *(n.)* 障礙，障礙物 |

| **635.** | social standing *(n.)* 社會地位 |

英文 Listen, in books they say that true love always faces obstacles. Either the lovers have different social standings or...

原句 *For aught that I could ever read, could ever hear by tale or history, the course of true love never did run smooth; but, either it was different in blood.*

中文 我在書上讀過，真愛總會面對考驗；不是因為門第不相當，就是……

《仲夏夜之夢》中的人文主義

　　《仲夏夜之夢》是一部集中體現文藝復興精神和人文主義思想的喜劇。雖然劇中的故事發生在古希臘時代，但人物的思想感情、道德標準卻完全以文藝復興時期英國現實的生活為依據。莎士比亞在劇中熱情地描繪資產階級新女性爭取自由戀愛、婚姻自主和反抗父權的情形，並通過現實與自然的對比，表達了人與人、人與自然和諧共處的人文主義理想。

636. thwart *(vt.)* 反對，阻撓，使受挫折

英文 If true lovers are always thwarted, then it must be a rule of fate.

原句 *If then true lovers have been ever crossed, it stands as an edict in destiny.*

中文 如果真心相愛的戀人永遠要遭受折磨，那也是命中注定的事。

●track *108*

637. a piece of *(ph.)* 一個，一張，一片，一塊，一齣，一則

英文 I am sure that it's a great piece of work and very funny.

原句 *A very good piece of work, I assure you, and a merry.*

中文 我敢說那是一齣好戲，而且很有趣。

638. believable *(adj.)* 可信的

英文 I'll have to cry to make my performance believable.

原句 *That will ask some tears in the true performing of it.*

中文 我必須在表演時掉下眼淚，才能讓演出逼真。

639. wear a mask *(ph.)* 戴面具

英文 You'll wear a mask, and you can make your voice as high as you want to.

原句 *You shall play it in a mask, and you may speak as small as you will.*

中文 你會戴著面具演出，所以你可以盡可能用細尖的聲音說台詞。

---

640. improvise *(vt.)* , *(vi.)* 即興創作，即興表演

英文 You can improvise the whole thing. It's just roaring.

原句 *You may do it extempore, for it is nothing but roaring.*

中文 你可以即興表演，只要吼叫幾聲就可以了。

---

641. ferociously *(adv.)* 兇猛地，非常地，驚人地

---

642. duchess *(n.)* 公爵夫人，女公爵

英文 If you roar too ferociously, you'll scare the duchess and the other ladies and make them scream.

原句 *An you should do it too terribly, you would fright the duchess and the ladies, that they would shriek.*

中文 如果你吼叫得太兇猛，就會嚇到公爵夫人和小姐們，讓她們尖叫出來。

643. bodyguard *(n.)* 護衛者，保鏢，護衛隊

英文 The tall cowslip flowers are her bodyguards.

原句 *The cowslips tall her pensioners be.*

中文 高高的櫻草是她的侍衛。

644. dewdrop *(n.)* 露珠

英文 Now I have to go find some dewdrops here and hang a pearl earring on every cowslip flower.

原句 *I must go seek some dewdrops here and hang a pearl in every cowslip's ear.*

中文 現在我要在這裡找一些露珠，然後給每株花櫻草掛上用露珠做的珍珠耳環。

645. elf *(n.)* 小精靈，頑皮的小孩

英文 The queen and her elves will be here soon.

原句 *Our queen and all our elves come here anon.*

中文 仙后和她的小精靈快要來了。

646. argue *(vt.)* 辯論，主張；*(vi.)* 辯論，爭吵，提出理由

647. acorn (*n.*) 橡子，橡實

英文 They always argue, and the little fairies get so frightened that they hide in acorn cups and won't come out.

原句 *But they do square, that all their elves for fear creep into acorn cups and hide them there.*

中文 他們見面就要爭吵架，小精靈們都嚇得躲進橡子殼不敢出來。

648. sneak (*vt.*) 偷竊，偷偷地做；(*vi.*) 偷偷地走；(*n.*) 告密者，溜走

649. shepherd (*vt.*) 牧羊，指導，護送，看管；(*n.*) 牧羊人

新女性的代表

　　《仲夏夜之夢》女主角荷米雅是莎士比亞筆下中產階級新女性的代表，她對父權制的勇敢抗爭傳達了新興中產階級對於女性地位和權利的重新考量。中世紀的教會對塑造社會的價值具有莫大的影響力，包括婦女的社會地位。教會聲稱女人是夏娃的後代，只會誘惑男人走向墮落，這一觀念瀰漫著整個中世紀時期。亨利八世繼位後，發動宗教改革運動，質疑對羅馬教會的信仰，教會對婦女的不公正態度也因而產生動搖。

650. play a pipe *(ph.)* 吹笛子

英文 But I know for a fact that you snuck away from Fairyland, disguised as a shepherd, spent all day playing straw pipes, and singing love poems to Phillida.

原句 *But I know when thou hast stolen away from Fairyland, and in the shape of Corin sat all day, playing on pipes of corn and versing love to amorous Phillida.*

中文 但是我知道你溜出仙境，假扮成牧羊人整天吹著麥笛，唱著情歌跟菲爾妲表達愛意。

651. get over *(ph.)* 克服，把……忘懷

652. give up *(ph.)* 讓出，放棄，戒掉

英文 Get over it. I won't give up this child for all of Fairyland.

原句 *Set your heart at rest. The Fairyland buys not the child of me.*

中文 你死心吧！我不會為仙境放棄這個孩子。

653. mortal *(adj.)* 會死的，凡人的，致命的；*(n.)* 凡人

654. give birth to *(ph.)* 生產，生育

655. for one's sake *(ph.)* 為了某人或某事物

英文 But since she was a mortal, she died giving birth to that boy, and for her sake I'm raising him and will let him keep me company forever.

原句 *But she, being mortal, of that boy did die; and for* *her sake do I rear up her boy, and for her sake I will not part with him.*

中文 不過她是一個凡人，在生產時死了。因為她的緣故我才會撫養這個男孩，而且絕不會捨棄他。

---

656. eyelid *(n.)* 眼皮，眼瞼

英文 If its juice is put on someone's eyelids while they're asleep, that person will fall in love with the next living creature he or she sees.

原句 *The juice of it on sleeping eyelids laid will make or man or woman madly dote upon the next live creature that it sees.*

中文 它的汁液如果滴在睡著的人的眼皮上，無論男女，醒來第一眼看見什麼生物，都會發瘋似愛上對方。

---

657. insult *(vt.)* 侮辱，羞辱

英文 Your behavior is an insult to all women.

原句 *Your wrongs do set a scandal on my sex.*

中文 你的行為對女性是種侮辱。

第一幕
第二景

●track *110*

---

658. yearn for *(ph.)* 盼望，思念，同情

英文 Love him and yearn for him, even if he's a cat, a bear, a leopard, or a wild boar.

原句 *Love and languish for his sake: be it ounce or cat or bear, pard or boar with bristled hair.*

中文 你會愛他、思念他，即使他是一隻貓、豹、熊，野豬。

---

659. faint *(vi.)* 昏厥，暈倒；*(adj.)* 頭暈的，微弱的，暗淡的；*(n.)* 昏厥

---

660. wander *(vt.)* , *(vi.)* , *(n.)* 漫遊，徘徊

英文 My love, you look like you're about to faint from wandering in the woods for so long, and to tell you the truth, I've gotten us lost.

原句 *Fair love, you faint with wandering in the woo; and to speak troth, I have forgot our way.*

中文 我的愛，因為在林中遊走，妳好像快昏倒了。不過老實說，我們迷路了。

---

661. remain *(vi.)* 剩下，保持，仍是

英文 I hope your love for me remains this strong for your entire life!

原句 *Thy love ne'er alter till thy sweet life end!*

中文 但願你對我的愛永保濃烈，直到你的生命盡頭！

---

662. soundly *(adv.)* 堅實地，酣暢地，徹底地

---

663. damp *(vt.)* 使潮濕；*(vi.)* 變潮濕；*(adj.)* 潮濕的；*(n.)* 濕氣，潮濕

英文 And here's the girl, sleeping soundly on the damp and dirty ground.

原句 *And here the maiden, sleeping sound, on the dank and dirty ground.*

中文 這就是那個少女，她正在潮濕骯髒的地上酣睡著。

---

664. out of breath *(ph.)* 上氣不接下氣，喘不過氣來

英文 Oh, I'm out of breath from this chase for love.

原句 *Oh, I am out of breath in this fond chase.*

中文 這場愛情的追逐讓我喘不過氣。

---

665. boring *(adj.)* 令人生厭的；乏味的

英文 I regret all the boring time I wasted with her.

原句 *I do repent the tedious minutes I with her have spent.*

中文 我後悔曾經跟她在一起虛度光陰。

---

666. harp on *(ph.)* 喋喋不休地談論

---

667. inadequacy *(n.)* 不適當，不充足

英文 Do you have to harp on my inadequacy?

原句 *But you must flout my insufficiency?*

中文 你需要這樣挖苦我的缺點嗎？

---

668. disdainful *(adj.)* 輕蔑的，驕傲的

英文 It's extremely wrong for you to woo me in such a cruel, disdainful way.

原句 *Good troth, you do me wrong, good sooth, you do, in such disdainful manner me to woo.*

中文 你真是對不起人，竟然用這种輕蔑的態度追求我。

---

669. shake *(vt.)* , *(vi.)* , *(n.)* 搖動，震動，握手

英文 Lysander, look how I'm shaking from fear.

原句 *Lysander, look how I do quake with fear.*

中文 賴桑德，你看我都嚇得發抖了。

● track *111*

---

670. rehearse *(vt.)* , *(vi.)* 排練，排演，練習

英文 This is the perfect place to rehearse.

原句 *And here's a marvelous convenient place for our rehearsal.*

中文 這是個排演的好地方。

---

671. leave out *(ph.)* 省去，遺漏

---

672. come to think of it *(ph.)* 仔細想一想，這樣一想

英文 I think we'll have to leave out all the killing, come to think of it.

原句 *I believe we must leave the killing out, when all is done.*

中文 想到這，我認為我們要刪掉自殺 (**killing** 在此句中意指自殺) 的情節。

673. a country bumpkin *(ph.)* 鄉巴佬，土包子

674. swagger *(vt.)* 威嚇；*(vi.)* , *(n.)* 昂首闊步，神氣活現

英文 Who are these country bumpkins swaggering around so close to where the fairy queen is sleeping?

原句 *What hempen homespuns have we swaggering here, so near the cradle of the fairy queen?*

中文 哪來的鄉巴佬在走動吵鬧，還離仙后臥榻那麼近？

675. have very little to do with *(ph.)* 與……關係不大

676. these days *(ph.)* 如今，當今

英文 But to tell you the truth, reason and love have very little to do with each other these days.

原句 *And yet, to say the truth, reason and love keep little company together nowadays.*

中文 不過說實在，這年頭很少人是因為理性地看到對方的德行，進而墜入戀情的。

---

677. depth *(n.)* 深度，厚度，深處

英文 I'll give you fairies as servants, and they'll bring you jewels from the depths of the ocean, and sing to you while you sleep on a bed of flowers.

原句 *I'll give thee fairies to attend on thee, and they shall fetch thee jewels from the deep, and sing, while thou on pressèd flowers dost sleep.*

中文 我會派小精靈們侍候你，他們會從海洋深處探取珍寶給你；當你在花床上睡去時，他們會唱歌給你聽。

---

678. moonbeam *(n.)* 月光

英文 Pluck off colorful butterfly wings, and use them to fan moonbeams away from his eyes as he sleeps.

原句 *And pluck the wings from painted butterflies to fan the moonbeams from his sleeping eyes.*

中文 折取彩蝶的翅膀，在他睡眠中用蝶翅把月光搧去。

---

679. bow *(vt.)* 弄彎；*(vi.)* 形成弓形，彎曲；*(n.)* 弓，蝴蝶結

---

680. curtsy *(vi.)* 行屈膝禮；*(n.)* 女子的屈膝禮

英文 Bow to him, fairies, and curtsy to him.

原句 *Nod to him, elves, and do him courtesies.*

中文 小精靈們，對他鞠躬後跟著敬禮吧！

---

681. **beg your pardon** *(ph.)* 請原諒，對不起

英文 I beg your pardon, sirs.

原句 *I cry your worships' mercy, heartily.*

中文 請各位先生多擔待。

---

682. **bandage** *(vt.)* 用繃帶包紮；*(n.)* 繃帶

英文 If I cut my finger, I'll use you as a bandage to stop the bleeding

原句 *If I cut my finger, I shall make bold with you.*

中文 假如我的手指頭割破的話，我就使用你 (此指蜘蛛網) 來止血。

第三幕
第二景

●track *112*

683. wonder *(vt.)* , *(vi.)* 納悶，想知道；*(n.)* 驚奇，奇蹟，奇觀

684. completely *(adv.)* 完整地；完全地；徹底地

685. in love with *(ph.)* 與……相愛

英文 I wonder if Titania is awake yet, and if she is, I wonder what the first thing she saw was. Whatever it is, she must be completely in love with it now.

原句 *I wonder if Titania be awaked; then, what it was that next came in her eye, which she must dote on in extremity.*

中文 不知道泰妲妮亞醒了沒；她一醒來，就會熱烈地愛上了她第一眼看到的任何生物。

686. worst *(adj.)* 最壞的，最惡劣的；*(adv.)* 最壞地，最惡劣地；*(n.)* 最壞者，最壞的部分

英文 Save that kind of harsh language for your worst enemy.

原句 *Lay breath so bitter on your bitter foe.*

中文 把這惡毒的話留給你的死敵。

687. reason *(vt.)* , *(vi.)* 推論，勸說；*(n.)* 理由，理性，推理

英文 I'm only scolding you now, but I should treat you much worse, because I'm afraid you've given me good reason to curse you.

原句 *Now I but chide, but I should use thee worse, for thou, I fear, hast given me cause to curse.*

中文 現在我不過罵你幾句而已；以後還要對你更壞，因為我覺得你有讓我咒詛你的理由。

---

688. would rather *(ph.)* 寧願，較喜歡

---

689. feed to *(ph.)* 以……餵養

英文 I would rather feed his corpse to my dogs.

原句 *I had rather give his carcass to my hounds.*

中文 我寧願把他的屍體拿來餵狗。

---

690. go after *(ph.)* 追求，追逐，追蹤

---

691. rage *(vi.)* 發怒，流行；*(n.)* 盛怒，風靡一時的事物

英文 I can't go after her when she's in a rage like this.

原句 *There is no following her in this fierce vein.*

中文 她這樣盛怒之下，我還是別跟著她。

---

692. illusion *(n.)* 錯覺，幻覺，幻想

英文 Bring her here with some trick or illusion, and I'll put the charm on his eyes when she comes.

原句 *By some illusion see thou bring her here: I'll charm his eyes against she do appear.*

中文 使一些法術把她引到這兒來，我要在她的眼睛施魔法。

---

693. sink into *(ph.)* 滲入，陷入

694. pupils *(n.)* 瞳孔，弟子，未成年人

英文 Let the juice of the purple flower, hit by Cupid's arrow, sink into the pupils of this man's eyes.

原句 *Flower of this purple dye, hit with Cupid's archery, sink in apple of his eye.*

中文 將曾被丘比特的弓箭射中的紫色小花，其具魔法的花液，滲進他的眼眸中。

695. ridiculous *(adj.)* 可笑的，滑稽的

英文 Should we watch this ridiculous scene? Lord, what fools these mortals are!

原句 *Shall we their fond pageant see? Lord, what fools these mortals be!*

中文 我們要不要觀賞一下他們的愛情鬧劇？老天，這些凡人真是蠢得可憐。

696. pursue *(vt.)* 追趕，追捕，追求，繼續；*(vi.)* 追趕，繼續

英文 Then the two of them will both pursue one girl.

原句 *Then will two at once woo one.*

中文 他們兩個同時追求一個女孩。

697. gang up *(ph.)* 聯合起來

英文 I see you're all determined to gang up on me for a few laughs.

原句 *I see you all are bent to set against me for your merriment.*

中文 我知道你們聯合起來取笑我。

| **698.** | provoke *(vt.)* 對……挑釁，煽動，導致 |

| **699.** | horrible *(adj.)* 可怕的，糟透的 |

| **700.** | teasing *(adj.)* 逗弄的，奚落的，挑逗的； *(n.)* 逗弄，奚落，挑逗 |

英文 Have you conspired with these two to provoke me with this horrible teasing?

原句 *Have you conspired, have you with these contrived to bait me with this foul derision?*

中文 妳和這些人一起設計這種糟糕的玩笑來嘲弄我嗎？

| **701.** | dumbfound *(vt.)* 使人驚愕失聲，使驚呆 |

英文 I'm completely dumbfounded by what you're saying.

原句 *I am amazèd at your passionate words.*

中文 妳說的話讓我太驚訝了。

| **702.** | on purpose *(ph.)* 故意地，為了 |

英文 This is all your fault. You make mistakes constantly, or else you cause this kind of trouble on purpose.

原句 *This is thy negligence: still thou mistakest, or else committ'st thy knaveries willfully.*

中文 這都是你的疏忽造成的；你要不是弄錯了，就一定是

故意搗蛋。

---

703. conflict *(n.)* 衝突，鬥爭，爭執

英文 When they wake up, all this trouble and conflict will seem like a dream or a meaningless vision.

原句 *When they next wake, all this derision shall seem a dream and fruitless vision.*

中文 等他們醒來，所有的錯誤和衝突，就會像是一場夢或是空虛的幻境。

● track *113*

---

704. caress *(vt.)* , *(n.)* 撫摸，撫抱

英文 Come over here and sit down on this flowery bed while I caress those lovable cheeks.

原句 *Come, sit thee down upon this flowery bed while I thy amiable cheeks do coy.*

中文 來，在這花床上坐下，我要撫摩你可愛的臉頰。

---

705. have a good ear for *(ph.)* 對⋯⋯有好的聽力

英文 I have a pretty good ear for music.

原句 *I have a reasonable good ear in music.*

中文 我對音樂很有好的鑑賞力。

706. go to sleep *(ph.)* 入睡

英文 Go to sleep, and I will wrap my arms around you.

原句 *Sleep thou, and I will wind thee in my arms.*

中文 去睡吧，我要把你環抱在臂中。

707. ranger *(n.)* 護林員

英文 One of you go find the forest ranger.

原句 *Go, one of you, find out the forester.*

中文 你們誰去把護林員找來。

708. somehow *(adv.)* 不知怎麼的，以某種方式

709. melt away *(ph.)* 融化，消失

豆 知識
浪漫穿越劇

　　《仲夏夜之夢》是超越時空的穿越劇。莎士比亞將整個故事安排在古希臘時代，但是其中人物的思想和語言的特色都是屬於伊利莎白文藝復興的時代，他這樣做的目的是為了不觸犯封建統治者又能表達自己的理想主義思想。這種構思使得莎士比亞在寫作時更能盡情發揮。另外，作者在劇情中也增加了屬於不同國家與時代的一些仙人和精靈，添加全劇的傳奇和浪漫色彩。

---

710. cheap *(adj.)* 便宜的，粗鄙的 *(adv.)* 便宜地，卑鄙地

英文 I'm not sure how it happened—but somehow, something made my love for Hermia melt away like snow. My past love for Hermia now seems like a memory of some cheap toy I used to love as a child.

原句 *But, my good lord, I wot not by what power—but by some power it is—my love to Hermia, melted as the snow, seems to me now as the remembrance of an idle gaud which in my childhood I did dote upon.*

中文 我不知道怎麼會這樣，但一定是有某種力量使我對荷米雅的愛情像雪一樣溶解了。現在想起來，那就像是童年時喜歡的玩具，只留下記憶而已。

---

711. for a time *(ph.)* 一度，曾經，暫時

---

712. natural *(adj.)* 正常的，自然的，天生的；*(n.)*
天然物，自然的事情

---

713. long for *(ph.)* 渴望

---

714. true to *(ph.)* 忠實於

英文 Then I hated her for a time, as a sick person hates the food he usually loves. But now I have my natural taste back, like a sick person when he recovers. Now I want Helena, I love her, I long for her, and I will always be true to her.

原句 *But like in sickness did I loathe this food; but, as in health, come to my natural taste, now I do wish it, love it, long for it, and will for evermore be true to it.*

中文 我一度很討厭荷米雅,但正如一個人生病時,對自己向來喜歡的食物沒胃口一樣,等到恢復健康,就會回復原來的胃口。現在我渴求她,珍愛她,思慕她,並將永遠對她忠心。

715.	couple *(vt.)* 連接,聯想;*(vi.)* 結合,成婚;*(n.)* 一對,夫婦,幾個

716.	sumptuous *(adj.)* 奢侈的,豪華的

英文 We three couples will celebrate with a sumptuous feast.

原句 *Three and three, we'll hold a feast in great solemnity.*

中文 我們三對佳偶,一起來舉行盛大的宴會。

717.	out of focus *(ph.)* 失焦,模糊

英文 It's like my eyes are out of focus, and I'm seeing everything double.

原句 *Methinks I see these things with parted eye, when everything seems double.*

中文 我覺得那就像是眼睛無法聚焦一樣,看什麼都是模糊重疊的。

718.	ballad *(n.)* 民謠,歌,情歌

英文 I'll get Peter Quince to write this dream down as a ballad.

原句 *I will get Peter Quince to write a ballad of this dream.*

中文 我要叫彼得昆斯為這個夢創作一首情歌。

● track *114*

719. kidnap *(vt.)* 誘拐，綁架，劫持

英文 I'm sure he's been kidnapped.

原句 *Out of doubt he is transported.*

中文 他準是被拐走了。

720. show up *(ph.)* 出現，揭露

英文 If he doesn't show up, the play is ruined.

原句 *If he come not, then the play is marred.*

中文 他要是不出現，這齣戲就沒辦法演了。

● track *115*

721. legend *(n.)* 傳說，傳說中的人或事，傳奇人物

英文 I'll never believe any of these old legends or fairy tales.

原句 *I never may believe these antique fables nor these fairy toys.*

中文 我從不相信這些古老的傳說和神話故事。

722.	lunatic *(adj.)* 瘋的，愚妄的；*(n.)* 瘋子

723.	overactive *(adj.)* 過於活躍的

英文 Lunatics, lovers, and poets all are ruled by their overactive imaginations.

原句 *The lunatic, the lover, and the poet are of imagination all compact.*

中文 瘋子、情人和詩人，都是想像的產物。

森林中的人性頓悟

　　在《仲夏夜之夢》中，莎士比亞對人性的深度頓悟，就像是一座莊嚴奇絕的大廈慢慢地顯現出來。劇中每個人都以為自己的欲望才是真實的，都認為是他人有意與自己為難，於是人與人之間毫無必要地競爭，造成了難以化解的現實危機。於是，莎士比亞構造出一座神奇的仲夏夜森林，讓飽受自以為是之苦的人進入其中看看人性的真實。當人能夠認識欲望的虛幻，才能夠正視自我並接受自我，超越攀比、嫉妒、虛榮乃至競爭。

724. Here's… *(ph.)* (用於句首，使人注意某人或某物)
瞧，在這裡，向這裡來

英文 Here's a list of all of the acts that have been prepared.

原句 *There is a brief, how many sports are ripe.*

中文 這裡有張單子列出可以演出的戲目。

725. last time *(ph.)* 上一次

726. conquer *(vt.)* 攻克，戰勝；*(vi.)* 得勝

英文 That's an old show, and I saw it the last time I came back from conquering Thebes.

原句 *That is an old device, and it was played when I from Thebes came last a conqueror.*

中文 那是齣舊戲碼，我上次從西比斯凱旋回來的時就已經表演過了。

727. critical *(adj.)* 緊要的，關鍵性的，吹毛求疵的

728. satire *(n.)* 諷刺，諷刺作品

英文 That's some sharp, critical satire, and it's not appropriate for a wedding.

原句 *That is some satire, keen and critical, not sorting with a nuptial ceremony.*

中文 那齣戲有些犀利、吹毛求疵，不適合婚禮時表演。

729. overburden *(vt.)* 使裝載過多，使負擔過重，
使過於勞累

730. try hard *(ph.)* 努力，力圖

英文 I don't like seeing poor people overburdened or looking bad when they're trying hard to do something good.

原句 *I love not to see wretchedness o'er charged, and duty in his service perishing.*

中文 我不歡喜看見可憐的人，做著他們能力所不及的事或努力想把事情做好卻失敗。

731. tongue-tied *(adj.)* 因驚嚇而說不出話的，緘默的

732. simplicity *(n.)* 簡單，簡樸，無知

733. in my opinion *(ph.)* 按照我的看法

英文 Therefore, love and tongue-tied simplicity can say the most even when they're saying the least, in my opinion.

原句 *Love, therefore, and tongue-tied simplicity in least speak most, to my capacity.*

中文 我的感想是，愛和木訥質樸的口才所說的話最少，但表達的意思卻最豐富的。

734. tangle *(vt.)* 使糾結，使捲入；*(vi.)*, *(n.)* 糾結

735. chain *(vt.)* 用鎖鏈拴住，拘禁；*(n.)* 鏈條，連鎖店

736. on and on *(ph.)* 繼續不停地

英文 His speech was like a tangled chain. It went on and on and was a total mess.

原句 *His speech was like a tangled chain. Nothing impaired, but all disordered.*

中文 他的話像是一段糾纏的鏈索，雖然沒有中斷，可是全弄亂了。

---

737. moan *(vt.)* 以呻吟聲說出，抱怨；*(vi.)* 呻吟，抱怨；*(n.)* 呻吟聲，發牢騷

英文 Oh wall, you've often heard me moaning because you keep me separated from my handsome Pyramus!

原句 *O Wall, full often hast thou heard my moans, for parting my fair Pyramus and me!*

中文 牆啊！你常常聽到我的呻吟，是因為你把我和俊俏的皮拉默思分開。

---

738. conscience *(n.)* 良心，道義心，善惡觀念

英文 Ah, it's a gentle animal, with a good conscience.

原句 *A very gentle beast, of a good conscience.*

中文 那是一隻不具傷害性的溫和動物。

---

739. wax *(vt.)* 給……上蠟；*(adj.)* 蠟製的；*(n.)* 蠟，石蠟

---

740. wane *(vi.)* 月虧，消逝，退潮；*(n.)* 月虧，衰退

英文 I'm tired of this moon. I wish he'd wax or wane off the stage.

原句 *I am aweary of this moon. Would he would change!*

中文 這厭倦這月亮，但願他可以有陰晴圓缺的變化！

741. beam *(vt.)* 以樑支撐，用……照射，流露；
(vi.) 照射，照耀；*(n.)* 樑，光線，光束

英文 Sweet Moon, I thank you for your sunny beams

原句 *Sweet Moon, I thank thee for thy sunny beams.*

中文 可愛的月亮，多謝你如陽光般的亮光。

742. chime *(vt.)* 和諧悅耳地奏出，用鐘聲報時；
(vi.) 鐘鳴，和諧，一致；*(n.)* 鐘樂，和諧，一致

英文 The clock has chimed midnight.

原句 *The iron tongue of midnight hath told twelve.*

中文 午夜的鐘聲已經敲了。

743. afraid *(adj.)* 害怕的，恐怕，擔心的

744. oversleep *(vt.)* , *(vi.)* 睡過頭

英文 I'm afraid we're going to oversleep in the morning as late as we've stayed up tonight.

原句 *I fear we shall outsleep the coming morn, as much as we this night have overwatched.*

中文 我擔心我們明天早晨會睡過頭，因為今天晚上睡得太晚。

第五幕
第一景

● track *116*

745. howl *(vt.)* 吼叫著說；*(vi.)*，*(n.)* 怒吼，號啕大哭，大笑

英文 Now the hungry lion roars and the wolf howls at the moon.

原句 *Now the hungry lion roars, and the wolf behowls the moon*

中文 現在飢餓的獅子在咆哮；豺狼對著月亮長嗥。

746. disturb *(vt.)*，*(vi.)* 妨礙，打擾

英文 I'm here to make sure that not even a mouse disturbs this blessed house.

原句 *Not a mouse shall disturb this hallowed house.*

中文 我確定連一隻老鼠都不會來擾亂這吉屋的清淨。

747. glimmer *(vi.)* 發出微光；*(n.)* 微光，少許

748. throughout *(adv.)* 處處，始終，在所有方面
(prep.) 遍及，貫穿，從頭到尾

英文 Let the dying fire shine a glimmering light throughout the house.

原句 *Through the house give glimmering light, by the dead and drowsy fire.*

中文 讓漸漸黯淡的爐火，以閃爍不定的微光照明整個屋內。

| 749. | applause *(n.)* 鼓掌，喝采，稱讚 |

| 750. | make up to *(ph.)* 補償，獻慇懃，巴結 |

英文 Give me some applause, if we're friends, and Robin will make everything up to you.

原句 *Give me your hands if we be friends, And Robin shall restore amends.*

中文 如果我們是朋友的話，請鼓鼓掌，羅賓會盡力報償各位的！

劇情簡介

《無事自擾》
(Much Ado About Nothing)

　　位於義大利西西里島東北角梅辛那城裡，唐佩德羅親王率領部下打勝仗歸來，正準備下榻在梅辛那城總督里歐納多 (Leonato) 的官邸，一行人的到來頓時讓總督的莊園顯得熱鬧非凡，莊嚴隆重的氣氛中透露著歡樂，更令人高興的是，這一天親王的親信克勞迪 (Claudio) 對里歐納多的女兒茜羅 (Hero) 一見鍾情，親王覺得是天大的喜事，便極力承諾要在化妝舞會上幫他向茜羅小姐求婚。

　　唐佩德羅親王的弟弟唐約翰 (Don John) 伯爵是位私生子，且是個搬弄是非的小人，他和親王哥哥之間一直存在隔閡，所以存心要破壞任何親王想要成就的事情，藉此和他作對並抒發他對人生境遇的不滿。於是他欺騙克勞迪，造謠說親王其實是在為自己求婚，因而讓克勞迪感到非常沮喪，不過，令人欣慰的是，克勞迪很快就發現事情的真相，一切是唐約翰伯爵從中作梗，婚禮依然會在一週後舉行。

　　大家都引頸期盼著婚禮的到來，但在等待的這段時間，親王很想促成部下班乃迪克 (Benedick) 和茜羅的表姐碧兒翠絲 (Beatrice) 的姻緣。班奈迪克是一個性情豪放又機智的年輕貴族，自負的他死守單身的主張，而碧兒翠絲則是一個性格活潑、伶牙俐齒的姑娘，兩個一見面，就要展開互相挖苦譏笑的唇槍舌戰。大家都看得出來他們是一對歡喜冤家，儘管一見面就吵嘴，但事實上，他們的個性十分相像而且彼此喜歡著對方，只是自己不知道而已。所以，親王策動大家私下幫他們傳話給對方，欺騙他們對方愛上自己了，而這個善意的謊言也果然奏效，讓他們漸漸滋生愛苗，最後終於由冤家變為夫妻。

　　正當官邸裏一片喜氣洋洋時，麻煩的事情又發生了，眼看婚禮即將要舉行，心懷不軌的唐約翰伯爵一計不成又施一計。由於他的部下曾和茜羅的女僕有染，於是他要求部下與女僕假裝是茜羅在茜羅房間的窗邊大聲談情，並故意將親王和克勞迪引到茜羅的窗下，使得他們相信茜羅是一個不值得克勞迪迎娶、水性楊花的風流女子。

　　婚禮上，克勞迪當眾羞辱茜羅，儘管茜羅和父親都感到冤屈，但這一次親王卻始終站在克勞迪一邊，無奈之下里歐納多只得對外宣稱茜羅因過度悲傷意外身亡。經過一番調查後，幕後黑手約翰伯爵逐漸浮出水面，事情真相大白，克勞迪為自己魯莽的行為悲痛不已，為求得里歐納多的原諒，他答應當眾向茜羅道歉，並迎娶里歐納多的侄女。當克勞迪揭開新娘的面紗時，他驚喜地

發現此刻站在他面前的就是心愛的茜羅，兩個人重歸於好，並在親王和眾人的祝福聲中，發誓要珍惜彼此一輩子。

● track *117*

---

751. greatly *(adv.)* 極其，大大地

---

752. expectation *(n.)* 期待，預期，前程

（英文）He has so greatly exceeded all expectations that I can't even describe all he's done.

（原句）*He hath indeed better bettered expectation than you must expect of me to tell you how.*

（中文）他的表現遠超過所有人的期待，那是言語無法形容的。

---

753. break out into tears *(ph.)* 突然開始哭起來

（英文）Did he break out into tears?

（原句）*Did he break out into tears?*

（中文）他有掉淚哭泣嗎？

---

754. display *(vt.)* 展覽，陳列，顯示；*(n.)* 展覽，陳列，顯示

（英文）That's a very natural display of affection.

原句 *A kind overflow of kindness.*

中文 這是情感的自然流露。

755. sincere *(adj.)* 衷心的，真誠的，正直的

英文 There's no face more sincere than one washed in tears.

原句 *There are no faces truer than those that are so washed.*

中文 淚洗的面孔是最真誠的。

756. put up *(ph.)* 建造，升起

757. a public notice *(ph.)* 公告

父權社會的無情

　　在父親統治的家長制社會中，女人是男人的財產，結婚之前屬於父親，結婚之後則屬於丈夫。《無事自擾》的女主角茜羅善良溫柔，受冤屈時卻不能為自己辯護，完全處於失語狀態。當茜羅在婚禮上被未婚夫克勞迪斥責不貞的時候，讓人為她叫屈，但為什麼茜羅不能為自己辯解呢？而茜羅的父親面對別人對茜羅「罪行」的指責，卻說了「對於她的羞恥，死是最好的遮掩」這樣的話，充分顯示父權統治社會的無情。

758. archery *(n.)* 射箭，箭術，弓箭手

英文 He once put up a public notice in Messina challenging Cupid to an archery match.

原句 *He set up his bills here in Messina and challenged Cupid at the flight.*

中文 他曾經在麥西納張貼公告，要和丘比特比賽射箭。

759. for God's sake *(ph.)* 看在上帝的份上

760. criticize *(vt.)* , *(vi.)* 批評，苛求，評論

761. get even with *(ph.)* 報復

英文 For God's sake, Beatrice, you're criticizing Signior Benedick too heavily, but I'm sure he'll get even with you.

原句 *Faith, niece, you tax Signor Benedick too much, but he'll be meet with you, I doubt it not.*

中文 天啊，碧兒翠絲，妳挖苦班乃迪克的話太過分了。不過，我敢說他不會饒過妳。

762. positively *(adv.)* 明確地，堅決地，正面地

英文 He's a lord to a lord and a man to a man. He is positively stuffed with honorable virtues.

原句 *A lord to a lord, a man to a man, stuffed with all honorable virtues.*

中文 他在貴族面前是貴族，在男子漢面前是男子漢。他十足充滿著高尚的美德。

---

763. fickle *(adj.)* 易變的，無常的

---

764. latest *(adj.)* 最新的，最近的；*(adv.)* 最近地；
(n.) 最新的事物

英文 He's incredibly fickle—his affection changes faster than the latest fashions.

原句 *He wears his faith but as the fashion of his hat; it ever changes with the next block.*

中文 他對人的情感非常善變，甚至比最新的流行時尚改變得更快。

---

765. run to *(ph.)* 達及，擴展到

英文 Most people choose to avoid trouble, but you run to it.

原句 *The fashion of the world is to avoid cost, and you encounter it.*

中文 大多數人躲避麻煩事，你卻自己迎上來。

---

766. mute *(vt.)* 消除聲音；*(vi.)* 沉默的，啞的；
(n.) 啞巴

英文 I can keep secrets like a mute.

原句 *I can be secret as a dumb man.*

中文 我可以像啞巴一樣保守祕密。

● track *118*

---

767. take care of *(ph.)* 照顧，留意，處理

英文 He is taking care of it.

原句 *He is very busy about it.*

中文 他正在處理那件事。

---

768. bright *(adj.)* 明亮的，歡快的，機靈的；*(adv.)* 明亮地，歡快地

英文 He's very bright.

原句 *A good sharp fellow.*

中文 他是個聰明機伶的人。

● track *119*

---

769. without limits *(ph.)* 無限制地

英文 Therefore my sadness is without limits.

原句 *Therefore the sadness is without limit.*

中文 所以我的憂傷沒有止境。

---

770. gloomy *(adj.)* 陰暗的，陰沉的，陰鬱的

英文 You should listen to reason. Then you'd stop being so gloomy.

原句 *You should hear reason.*

中文 你應該聽從理性，這樣就不會如此憂鬱。

---

771. hedge *(vt.)* 用樹籬笆圍住；*(vi.)* 修築樹籬；
(n.) 樹籬，籬笆

英文 I'd rather be a multiflora rose in a hedge than a rose in my brother's garden.

原句 *I had rather be a canker in a hedge than a rose in his grace.*

中文 我寧願是樹籬旁的野薔薇，也不要成為我哥哥花園中的玫瑰。

---

772. musty *(adj.)* 發霉的，有霉味的

---

773. in the middle of *(ph.)* 在……當中

英文 As I was working on one musty room, the Prince and Claudio entered. They were in the middle of a serious conversation.

原句 *As I was smoking a musty room, comes me the Prince and Claudio, hand in hand, in sad conference.*

中文 當我在一間發霉的房間做工時，親王和克勞迪走進來，並且談著重要的事情。

774. spoil *(vt.)* 損壞，糟蹋，寵壞；*(vi.)* 食物變壞，腐敗；*(n.)* 掠奪物

775. overjoy *(vt.)* 使狂喜

英文 If there's any way I can spoil his life, I'll be overjoyed.

原句 *If I can cross him any way, I bless myself every way.*

中文 假如可以破壞他的生活，我一定會很快樂。

●track *120*

776. sour *(adj.)* 酸的，脾氣壞的，刻薄的

777. heartburn *(n.)* 胃灼熱，心痛，妒忌

英文 That man always looks so sour! Just looking at him gives me heartburn.

原句 *How tartly that gentleman looks! I never can see him but I am heartburned an hour after.*

中文 他看起來一副尖酸刻薄樣，我每次看到他就感到胃不舒服。

778. ill-tempered *(adj.)* 壞脾氣的，易怒的

英文 Honestly, she is too ill-tempered.

原句 *In faith, she's too curst.*

中文 沒錯，她脾氣太壞了。

779. defer to *(ph.)* 聽從

英文 I trust that you will defer to your father on these important decisions.

原句 *I trust you will be ruled by your father.*

中文 我相信你會聽從你父親的話。

780. romance *(n.)* 中世紀騎士故事，傳奇小說，愛情小說，戀愛

781. timing *(n.)* 計時，時間的安排

英文 If he is too insistent, tell him that romance is like a dance: it has its own rhythm and timing.

原句 *If the Prince be too important, tell him there is measure in everything, and so dance out the answer.*

中文 假如親王很堅持，妳就告訴他愛情就像舞蹈有其該有的節奏和時間。

782. stage *(n.)* 舞臺，階段，時期

783. repent *(vt.)* , *(vi.)* 悔悟，悔改

784. jig *(n.)* 吉格舞

785. cinquepace *(n.)* 一種輕快的舞曲

英文 Look, the three stages of romance are like three different dances. Wooing, wedding, and repenting is as a Scotch jig, a classical dance, and a cinquepace.

(原句) *For hear me, Hero, wooing, wedding, and repenting is as a Scotch jig, a measure, and a cinquepace.*

(中文) 聽我說，愛情的三個階段就像三種舞步：求婚像蘇格蘭快步舞；結婚是莊嚴的舞；婚後的悔恨是輕快的舞曲。

786. whimsy *(n.)* 反覆無常，異想天開

(英文) The wooing is like a Scottish jig: hot and fast and full of whimsy and illusion.

(原句) *The first suit is hot and hasty like a Scotch jig, and full as fantastical.*

(中文) 求婚像蘇格蘭快步舞熱烈而急切的，且充滿奇思幻想。

787. decorous *(adj.)* 有禮貌的，端正的

(英文) The wedding is like a dance you would do before the King: proper and decorous.

(原句) *The wedding, mannerly modest as a measure, full of state and ancientry*

(中文) 結婚像是在宮殿中跳舞，舞步高尚且優雅。

788. eventually *(adv.)* 最後，終於

789. topple over *(ph.)* 倒塌，推翻，顛覆

(英文) Repenting is like the lively cinquepace: it goes faster and faster until you eventually topple over and die.

(原句) *And then comes repentance, and with his bad legs, falls into the cinquepace faster and faster, till he sink into his grave.*

中文 後悔像是快步舞，越跳越快直到倒下，最後終將死去。

---

790. in broad daylight *(ph.)* 光天化日，大白天

英文 I can see a church in broad daylight.

原句 *I can see a church by daylight.*

中文 我在大白天時可以看到教堂。

---

791. partygoer *(n.)* 社交聚會常客

英文 The partygoers have arrived.

原句 *The revelers are entering, brother.*

中文 參加宴會的人來了。

---

792. imitate *(vt.)* 模仿，模擬

英文 You could only imitate his imperfections so well if you were the man himself.

原句 *You could never do him so ill-well unless you were the very man.*

中文 除非你是他本人，不然不可能模仿他的缺點這麼逼真。

---

793. happen a lot *(ph.)* 經常發生

---

794. occur to *(ph.)* 被想起，被想到

英文 Beauty is a witch whose spells can turn loyalty into passion. This happens a lot, but it didn't occur to me that it would happen to me.

原句 *Beauty is a witch against whose charms faith melteth into blood. This is an accident of hourly proof, which I mistrusted not.*

中文 美貌是個女巫，會將忠貞變成情欲。這是經常會發生的事，我竟然沒想到會發生在我身上。

795. severely *(adv.)* 嚴格地，嚴厲地，嚴重地

英文 She mocks all her suitors so severely that they drop the suit.

原句 *She mocks all her wooers out of suit.*

中文 她嚴厲地嘲諷每個追求者，使得他們放棄求婚。

第二幕
第二景

●track *121*

796. blatant *(adj.)* 明顯的，露骨的，公然的

797. certainty *(n.)* 確實，必然的事

798. call off *(ph.)* 取消

英文 It'll be such blatant evidence of Hero's disloyalty that Claudio's jealousy will quickly turn to certainty, and the wedding will be instantly called off.

原句 *In the meantime I will so fashion the matter that Hero shall be absent, and there shall appear such seeming truth of Hero's disloyalty that jealousy shall be called assurance, and all the preparation overthrown.*

中文 把茜羅的背叛弄得像真的一般，讓克勞迪產生猜忌，如此一來，婚禮就會辦不成。

● track *122*

799. to the point *(ph.)* 中肯，恰當，扼要

800. elaborate *(vt.)* 精心製作，詳盡闡述；*(vi.)* 詳細說明，詳盡計畫

英文 He used to speak plainly and to the point, like an honorableman and soldier; now his speech is elaborate and flowery.

原句 *He was wont to speak plain and to the purpose, like an honest man and a soldier; and now is he turned orthography.*

中文 他過去説話簡潔、切中要點，像一個正直的人和軍人；現在他變得講話會咬文嚼字。

801. divine *(adj.)* 神的，神性的，神聖的

802. captivate *(vt.)* 使著迷，蠱惑

英文 That music must be divine, because his soul has been captivated.

原句 *Now, divine air! Now is his soul ravished.*

中文 這是神聖的音樂，他為之神往了。

803. invincible *(adj.)* 無敵的，不屈不撓的

804. assault *(vt.)* 攻擊，襲擊；*(vi.)* 動武；*(n.)* 攻擊，襲擊

英文 I would have thought she was invincible against any assault of love.

原句 *I would have thought her spirit had been invincible against all assaults of affection.*

中文 我以為她的心不會遭受任何愛情的攻擊。

805. smug *(adj.)* 沾沾自喜的；*(n.)* 沾沾自喜的人

英文 They say I'll be smug if I find out she loves me.

原句 *They say I will bear myself proudly if I perceive the love come from her.*

中文 他們說如果我發現她愛我，就會沾沾自喜。

豆知識
不做男性附屬物的女人

　　《無事自擾》中女主角茜羅的堂姐碧兒翠絲和靜默的茜羅是個明顯的對比。碧兒翠絲能言善辯且打破常規，拒絕接受社會結構中的女性地位，不願找個丈夫來養活她。碧兒翠絲極具個性，她可以公開和男人們辯論、鬥智鬥勇，用機智的謊言將婚姻拒之門外，她不畏權貴，不願做男性的附屬物。很明顯地，莎士比亞透過這個角色傳達出對父權王權制社會的不滿。

806. eavesdrop *(vi.)* 偷聽，偷聽

英文 She can hide there and eavesdrop on our conversation.

原句 *There will she hide her to listen our propose.*

中文 她會躲起來偷聽我們說話。

807. the best part of *(ph.)* 絕大部分，最好的部分

808. cut through *(ph.)* 克服，抄近路

809. greedily *(adv.)* 貪心地，貪婪地，貪吃地

英文 The best part of fishing is watching the fish cut through the water and greedily take the bait.

原句 *The pleasant'st angling is to see the fish cut with her golden oars the silver stream and greedily devour the treacherous bait.*

中文 釣魚最大的樂趣是，看著魚逆著水流，貪婪地吃著魚餌上鉤。

810. encourage *(vt.)* 鼓勵，慫恿，激發

811. wedding band *(ph.)* 結婚戒指

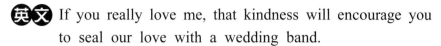

英文 If you really love me, that kindness will encourage you to seal our love with a wedding band.

原句 *If thou dost love, my kindness shall incite thee to bind our loves up in a holy band.*

中文 假如你真的愛我，我的好意將會鼓勵你用婚姻來證明我們的愛情。

●track *124*

---

812. clapper *(n.)* 鐘擺

英文 His heart is like a bell, with his tongue as the clapper: everything his heart thinks, and then his tongue speaks.

原句 *He hath a heart as sound as a bell, and his tongue is the clapper, for what his heart thinks, his tongue speaks.*

中文 他的心像是一個鐘，舌頭便是鐘擺；他內心想到什麼，就說什麼。

---

813. urge *(vt.)* 催促，激勵，極力主張；*(vi.)* 極力主張；*(n.)* 強烈的慾望，推動力

英文 If there's any reason we shouldn't get married, I urge you to tell me.

原句 *If there be any impediment, I pray you discover it.*

中文 要是有任何理由我們不應該結婚，我求你告訴我。

---

814. represent *(vt.)* 表現，象徵，表示，作為……的代表；
(vi.) 代表

英文 The word is too good to represent her wickedness.

原句 *The word is too good to paint out her wickedness.*

中文 這樣說還不足以形容她的邪惡。

---

815. shame *(vt.)* 使感到羞恥；*(n.)* 羞辱，憾事，
令人憎惡的事

---

816. congregation *(n.)* 集合，會集

英文 If I see anything tonight that convinces me not to marry her, I'll shame her tomorrow in the very congregation where I would have married her.

原句 *If I see anything tonight why I should not marry her, tomorrow in the congregation, where I should wed, there will I shame her.*

中文 假如我今晚看到任何足以讓我明天拒絕跟她結婚的事，我明天就會在婚禮上當眾羞辱她。

● track 125

817. gift (n.) 禮物，天賦，才能

英文 To be good-looking is a matter of luck, but to read and write is a natural gift.

原句 *To be a well-favored man is the gift of fortune, but to write and read comes by nature.*

中文 相貌漂亮是運氣好，但是讀寫的能力則需要天賦的才情。

818. subject (n.) 王子，親王，君主

英文 If he won't stop when he's told to, then he isn't one of the Prince's subjects.

原句 *If he will not stand when he is bidden, he is none of the Prince's subjects.*

中文 假如你要他站住而他繼續走，那麼他就不是親王的臣民。

819. merciful (adj.) 仁慈的，寬容的

英文 You have always been known as a merciful man, partner.

原句 *You have been always called a merciful man, partner.*

中文 你一直被認為是個寬大的人。

820. seduce (vt.) 誘惑，引誘

英文 But I will tell you that I seduced Margaret, the Lady Hero's waiting woman, tonight. I will call her "Hero" the whole time.

原句 *But know that I have tonight wooed Margaret, the Lady Hero's gentlewoman, by the name of Hero.*

中文 告訴你我今晚會引誘茜羅小姐的侍女，而且我會一直稱呼她為「茜羅」。

---

821. imfamous *(adj.)* 聲名狼藉的，罪大惡極的，不名譽的

---

822. commonwealth *(n.)* 全體公民，國家，共和國

英文 We have revealed the most imfamous love affair that was ever known in the commonwealth.

原句 *We have here recovered the most dangerous piece of lechery that ever wasknown in the commonwealth.*

中文 我們發現了國內有史以來最聲名狼藉的的背叛。

豆 知識 精準掌握角色心理變化

　　《無事自擾》充分展示莎士比亞對劇中人物喜劇心理的高超把握，並且按照自然邏輯來佈局人物情感的變化，表現出十分嫻熟的創造才能，使得此劇成為意味雋永之作。另外，《無事自擾》的創造性不僅體現在心理變化的精準掌握，更表現出不同以往的喜劇特色，以謊言與真實之間的錯位來營造濃郁的喜劇效果。

823. wig *(vt.)* 使戴假髮；*(n.)* 假髮

824. headdress *(n.)* 頭飾；頭巾

英文 I like your new wig and headdress, though I'd like it more if the hair were a shade browner.

原句 *I like the new tire within excellently, if the hair were a thought browner.*

中文 我喜歡妳的新假髮和頭飾，不過如果髮色再深一些，會更漂亮。

825. no better than *(ph.)* 實際上和……一樣

英文 Compared to your dress, it's no better than a nightgown.

原句 *By my troth, 's but a nightgown in respect of yours.*

中文 和妳的禮服比起來，那只能算是件睡衣。

●track *127*

---

826. become *(vt.)* 適合，同……相稱；*(vi.)* 變成，變得

---

827. tedious *(adj.)* 冗長乏味的，使人厭煩的

英文 Partners, you are becoming tedious.

原句 *Neighbors, you are tedious.*

中文 夥伴們，你們太聒噪了。

---

828. examine *(vt.)* 檢查，細查，審問；*(vi.)* 檢查，調查

---

829. findings *(n.)* 發現，發現物，調查結果

英文 Examine them yourselves, then bring me your findings.

原句 *Take their examination yourself and bring it me.*

中文 你們自己審問他們，然後再告訴我結果。

---

830. inkwell *(n.)* (嵌在桌子或墨水臺上的) 墨水池

英文 Tell him to bring his pen and his inkwell to the jail.

原句 *Bid him bring his pen and inkhorn to the jail.*

中文 告訴他帶筆和墨水池到監獄來。

272

● track *128*

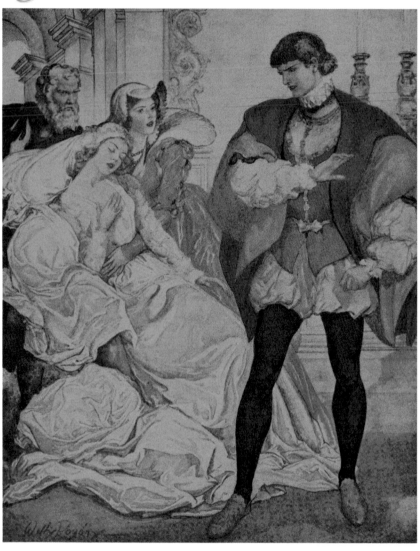

---

831. rising *(adj.)* 上升的，增大的，成長中的

---

832. suggest *(vt.)* 建議，提議，暗示

英文 Doesn't that rising blush suggest that she is virtuous and innocent?

原句 *Comes not that blood as modest evidence to witness simple virtue?*

中文 她臉上的紅暈，不正是純潔美德的證明？

---

833. tempt *(vt.)* 引誘，勾引，打動

---

834. indecent *(adj.)* 下流的，粗鄙的，不適當的

---

835. modest *(adj.)* 謙虛的，適度的，有節制的

---

836. sincerity *(n.)* 真實，誠心誠意

英文 I never seduced her, or tempted her with indecent words. I treated her like a brother would treat a sister, with modest sincerity and appropriate affection.

原句 *I never tempted her with word too large; but, as a brother to his sister, showed bashful sincerity and comely love.*

中文 我從未用放肆的話去引誘她，我對待她像妹妹般，給予適度的真情和合宜的愛意。

---

837. authority *(n.)* 權力，權威人士，專家

838. order *(vt.)*, *(vi.)* 命令，指揮；*(n.)* 命令，順序，有條理，訂購

839. truthfully *(adv.)* 深信不疑地，信任地

英文 Let me just ask her one question, and by your authority as her father, order her to answer truthfully.

原句 *Let me but move one question to your daughter; and by that fatherly and kindly power that you have in her, bid her answer truly.*

中文 讓我問她一個問題，請您以父親的權威，命令她誠實回答。

840. stain *(vt.)* 沾汙，敗壞；*(vi.)* 變髒，被沾汙；*(n.)* 汙點，汙跡

841. a just accusation *(ph.)* 公正的指責

英文 Who can stain that name with a just accusation?

原句 *Who can blot that name with any just reproach?*

中文 誰能夠用公正的指責來玷汙這個名字？

842. revelation *(n.)* 揭示，天啟，神示

英文 These revelations have overwhelmed her.

原句 *These things, come thus to light, smother her spirits up.*

中文 東窗事發讓她承受不了。

843. tear apart *(ph.)* 撕碎，撕開，拆散

844. bare *(vt.)* 使赤裸，揭露；*(adj.)* 裸的

英文 If they have spoken the truth about Hero, I will tear her apart with my bare hands.

原句 *If they speak but truth of her, these hands shall tear her.*

中文 假如他們所說關於茜羅的事都是真的，我會親自撕碎她。

845. nothing in the world *(ph.)* 世界上沒有任何事物

英文 There is nothing in the world that I love as much as you. Isn't that strange?

原句 *I do love nothing in the world so well as you: is not that strange?*

中文 這世界上我最愛的就是妳，這是不是很不可思議？

第四幕
第一景

● track *129*

846. malefactor *(n.)* 作惡者，罪犯

英文 Which ones are the malefactors?

原句 *Which be the malefactors?*

中文 誰是罪人？

847. criminal *(adj.)* 犯罪的，犯法的；*(n.)* 罪犯

848. for certain *(ph.)* 確定地，肯定地

英文 Gentlemen, it's already been proven that you aren't much better than lying criminals, and soon we'll know almost for certain.

原句 *Masters, it is proved already that you are little better than false knaves, and it will go near to be thought so shortly.*

中文 先生們，那已經證明你們比詐欺的惡人好不了多少，而且不久就可確認了。

849. come over here *(ph.)* 過來這裡

英文 Come over here; I'll whisper a word in your ear.

原句 *Come you hither, sirrah, a word in your ear.*

中文 你過來，我要在你耳邊說句話。

850. everlasting *(adj.)* 永遠的，永久的，不朽的

851. redemption *(n.)* 贖回，償還，救贖

英文 You'll be condemned to everlasting redemption for this.

原句 *Thou wilt be condemned into everlasting redemption for this.*

中文 為了這件事，你會受詛咒要一輩子贖罪。

852. exactly *(adv.)* 確切地，完全地，恰好地

853. on the spot *(ph.)* 立即，當場

854. grief *(n.)* 悲痛，不幸，災難

英文 Hero was accused exactly as the watchman described, and died on the spot from the grief.

原句 *Hero was in this manner accused, in this very manner refused, and upon the grief of this, suddenly died.*

中文 茜羅就是像侍衛所描述的那樣被控訴，而且當場就因悲傷而死。

855. tie…up *(ph.)* 捆綁，阻礙，密切相關

英文 Come on, tie them up.

原句 *Come, bind them.*

中文 來人，把他們綁起來。

第五幕
第一景

•track *130*

856. carry on *(ph.)* 繼續，進行，經營

英文 If you carry on the way you've been doing, you'll kill yourself.

原句 *If you go on thus, you will kill yourself.*

中文 如果你繼續這樣下去，會害死你自己。

---

857. in a hurry *(ph.)* 迅速地，匆忙地

英文 We're in a bit of a hurry, Leonato.

原句 *We have some haste, Leonato.*

中文 我們走得有點太倉促，里歐納多。

---

858. intimidate *(vt.)* 威嚇，脅迫

英文 Don't bother trying to intimidate me by putting your hand on your sword.

原句 *Nay, never lay thy hand upon thy sword.*

中文 用不著把手按在劍上試圖嚇我。

---

859. go for *(ph.)* 去拿，爭取，贊成，選擇

英文 Really, I had no intention of going for my sword.

原句 *In faith, my hand meant nothing to my sword.*

中文 老實說，我把手按在劍上沒有什麼用意。

---

860. constable *(n.)* 警官

---

861. too...to *(ph.)* 太……而不能

---

862. brilliant *(adj.)* 光輝的，傑出的，優秀的

英文 This educated constable is too brilliant for me to understand.

原句 *This learned constable is too cunning to be understood.*

中文 這位有教養的警官太聰明了，我無法了解他。

---

863. foundation *(n.)* 創建，基金會，機構

英文 God save the foundation!

原句 *God save the foundation!*

中文 上帝保佑這個團體！(此句為乞丐答謝宗教團體施捨的慣用語)

● track *131*

---

864. sonnet *(n.)* 十四行詩

---

865. praise *(vt.)* , *(vi.)* 讚揚，稱讚

英文 Afterward, will you write a sonnet for me, praising my beauty?

原句 *Will you then write me a sonnet in praise of my beauty?*

中文 那麼接著你可以寫一首十四行詩，讚美我的美貌嗎？

---

866. nauseate *(vt.)* 對⋯⋯感到噁心，使感到噁心；
(vi.) 作嘔，厭惡

英文 If you had foul words in your mouth, then your breath must be foul, and foul breath is nauseating.

原句 *Foul words is but foul wind, and foul wind is but foul breath, and foul breath is noisome.*

中文 假如你口出惡言，那麼你的口中的氣息就會是臭的，

這種不好的氣息很噁心。

---

867. lap *(n.)* 膝部，重疊部分

---

868. what's more *(ph.)* 另外，而且.

英文 I will live in your heart, die in your lap, and be buried in your eyes—and, what's more, I will go with you to your uncle's.

原句 *I will live in thy heart, die in thy lap, and be buried in thy eyes; and moreover, I will go with thee to thy uncle's.*

中文 我要住在你心裏、死在你的懷裏、葬在你的眼裏。還有，我會和妳起去妳伯父家。

第五幕
第三景

● track *132*

---

869. tomb *(n.)* 墓，墳地，死亡

英文 Is this the family tomb of Leonato?

原句 *Is this the monument of Leonato?*

中文 這是里歐納多家族的墳墓嗎？

---

870. epitaph *(n.)* 墓志銘，碑文

英文 This epitaph will hang here forever, continuing to praise Hero after I die.

原句 *Hang thou there upon the tomb, praising her when I am dumb.*

中文 這個墓誌銘會永遠懸掛在這裡，在我死後繼續頌禱她。

第五幕
第四景

●track *133*

---

871. unintentionally *(adv.)* 非故意地，非存心地

英文 Margaret is partially guilty, although our investigation shows that she acted unintentionally.

原句 *But Margaret was in some fault for this, although against her will, as it appears in the true course of all the question.*

中文 不過瑪格麗特也有一些過失，雖然調查發現她不是故意的。

---

872. sort out *(ph.)* 挑出，分開，解決

英文 Well, I'm glad that everything has been sorted out.

原句 *Well, I am glad that all things sort so well.*

中文 好，我很高興事情都解決了。

---

873. puzzled *(adj.)* 困惑的，搞糊塗的，茫然的

英文 Sir, I'm puzzled by what you just said.

原句 *Your answer, sir, is enigmatical.*

中文 大人，我無法理解你說的話。

874. giddy *(adj.)* 暈眩的，眼花的

875. flighty *(adj.)* 不負責任的；充滿幻想的

英文 Man is a giddy, flighty thing: that's my conclusion.

原句 *For man is a giddy thing, and this is my conclusion.*

中文 人是脆弱善變的，這就是我的結論。

不一樣的喜劇風格

　　《無事自擾》的喜劇情節與喜劇色彩，在於人物的性格和人物的心理。莎士比亞絕妙地利用劇中角色編織的虛而不實的假象，讓人物角色展開性格和心理的互相糾葛，從而產生出妙趣橫生的喜劇感，莎士比亞讓人物自身去虛構各種情景，用心理去感應、去醞釀出喜劇情境。這是此劇最大的特色，展示出了不同的喜劇風格。

劇情簡介

《第十二夜》
(Twelfth Night)

　　伊利里亞王國的貴族奧西諾 (Orsino)，因思念奧莉維亞 (Olivia) 而日益消瘦。但他無法擁有她，因為她哀悼過世的哥哥而拒絕所有的求婚。

　　這時，由於海上暴風雨造成船難，一名年輕的女貴族薇歐拉 (Viola)，被暴風雨沖上伊利里亞的岸邊。醒來時，她發現自己孤單地身處異地，推測雙胞胎哥哥賽巴斯丁 (Sebastian) 可能已在船難中被淹沒了。但傷心之餘，她仍然要養活自己，一位親切的船長告訴她關於奧西諾和奧莉維亞的故事，吸引了她，因此她希望能到奧莉維亞家中工作，但是奧莉維亞拒絕與陌生人談話，所以她無法如願找到工作。最後她化名舍沙里歐，喬裝成男人，才在奧西諾公爵家中找到侍從的職務。

　　佯裝成男人的薇歐拉立即成為奧西諾寵愛的僕役，並且愛上奧西諾，但奧西諾一直以為她是男人。當奧西諾請舍沙里歐送情書給奧莉維亞時，她立即愛上了年輕

的舍沙里歐。因而形成難解的三角關係：薇歐拉愛奧西諾，奧西諾愛奧莉維亞，而奧莉維亞卻愛舍沙里歐。

其實，賽巴斯丁還活著，但他誤以為妹妹已經死了，便與他的朋友兼保護者安東尼歐一起到達伊利里亞。自從船難後，安東尼歐一直熱情地照料著賽巴斯丁，同時也跟隨他來到他的敵人奧西諾的領土上。

奧莉維亞的仰愛慕者安德魯發覺奧莉維亞對舍沙里歐的愛，便向舍沙里歐挑戰決鬥。然而，當賽巴斯丁(神似男裝的薇歐拉)一出現，安德魯以為賽巴斯丁就是舍沙里歐，便與他打鬥。此時，奧莉維亞在打鬥的混亂之中到來，遇到賽巴斯丁，也誤以為他就是舍沙里歐，要求他與她結婚。賽巴斯丁感到十分困惑，因為他從未見過她，然而，看到她如此美麗，便樂意地答應她的要求。

另一方面，安東尼歐卻遭到奧西諾官員拘捕，但因為他誤以為舍沙里歐是賽巴斯丁，便要求其幫助脫困。不過舍沙里歐否認認識安東尼歐，使得安東尼歐被官員帶走，他大罵賽巴斯丁背叛他。當聽到哥哥的名字，舍沙里歐內心燃起希望，認為哥哥也許還活在世上。

後來，舍沙里歐和奧西諾起身前往奧莉維亞的住處，奧莉維亞看到舍沙里歐十分高興，以為他就是與他剛結婚的丈夫賽巴斯丁，看到如此的情境，奧西諾十分憤怒，但當賽巴斯丁出現時，真相終於大白。賽巴斯丁與薇歐拉終於快樂團聚，而奧西諾也發現薇歐拉原來是女扮男裝，他由於深愛著她，便向她求婚。

第一幕
第一景

● track 134

876. breeze (vi.) 吹著微風；(n.) 微風，和風

877. a bank of (ph.) 一排，一組，一堆，一團

878. scent (vt.) 嗅出，聞到，使充滿氣味；(vi.)
發出氣味；(n.) 氣味，香味，香水

英文 Oh, it sounded like a sweet breeze blowing gently over a bank of violets, spreading the pleasant scent around.

原句 *Oh, it came o'er my ear like the sweet sound, that breathes upon a bank of violets, stealing and giving odor.*

中文 啊，那音樂像吹過一片紫羅蘭的悅人微風，送來一股芳香。

879. go hunting (ph.) 去打獵

英文 Do you want to go hunting, my lord?

原句 *Will you go hunt, my lord?*

中文 大人，您要去打獵嗎？

880. instant (adj.) 立即的，緊迫的，速食的，即溶的；
(n.) 頃刻，一剎那

881. hart *(n.)* 雄鹿

882. a pack of *(ph.)* 一包、一盒、一箱、一群

883. vicious *(adj.)* 邪惡的，墮落的，惡毒的

英文 In that instant, I was transformed into a hart, and my desire for her has hounded me like a pack of vicious dogs.

原句 *That instant was I turned into a hart, and my desires, like fell and cruel hounds, e'er since pursue me.*

中文 在那瞬間，我變成了一隻雄鹿，而我的期望則像是一群兇惡的獵狗，一直在追著我。

《第十二夜》

　　《第十二夜》是唯一一部有另外一個劇名的莎士比亞作品，又名《隨心所欲》（What you will）。《第十二夜》得名於西方的傳統節日，基督教聖誕假期中的最後一夜為第十二夜，也就是一月六日的「主顯節」（Epiphany）。不過劇本中並沒有任何與這個節日或聖誕節有關的內容。這是因為伊莉莎白時期的英國，「主顯節」已經演變成狂歡作樂的日子，這個劇名暗示著一個脫離現實的嘉年華世界，任何離奇的事件都不需要合理的解釋。

● track *135*

---

884. fluke *(vt.)* , *(vi.)* , *(n.)* 僥倖

英文 It was a total fluke that you yourself were saved.

原句 *It is perchance that you yourself were saved.*

中文 妳自己也是僥倖獲救的。

---

885. custody *(n.)* 照管，監護，監禁

---

886. swear off *(ph.)* 發誓戒除

---

887. in memory of *(ph.)* 紀念

英文 Her brother had custody of her for a while, but then he died too. They say she's totally sworn off men now, in memory of her brother.

原句 *In the protection of his son, her brother, who shortly also died, for whose dear love, they say, she hath abjured the company and sight of men.*

中文 她的哥哥照顧她一段時間後也去世了。據說她為了悼念兄長，從此不肯會見男人。

---

888. plenty *(adj.)* 很多的，足夠的 *(n.)* 豐富，充足，大量

---

889. conceal *(vt.)* 隱蔽，隱藏，隱瞞

英文 Please—and I'll pay you plenty for this—help me conceal my identity, and find me the right disguise so I can look the way I want.

原句 *I prithee—and I'll pay thee bounteously—conceal me what I am, and be my aid for such disguise as haply shall become the form of my intent.*

中文 我請求你幫助我喬裝隱藏身分，我會付給你豐富報酬的。

●track *136*

---

890. **destroy** *(vt.)* 毀壞，消滅，希望破滅

英文 You're going to destroy yourself with all this drinking.

原句 *That quaffing and drinking will undo you.*

中文 你這樣喝酒會把你毀了。

---

891. average *(adj.)* 平均的，一般的，普通的；
(n.) 平均，一般，普通

英文 Sometimes I think I'm no smarter than average.

原句 *Methinks sometimes I have no more wit than a Christian or an ordinary man has.*

中文 有時候我覺得自己比不上一般人聰明。

---

892. accomplishment *(n.)* 完成，實現，成就，才藝

英文 Is this the kind of world where we hide our accomplishments?

原句 *Is it a world to hide virtues in?*

中文 身處現在的世界，需要我們隱藏才藝嗎？

---

893. throw a party *(ph.)* 舉行宴會、酒會

英文 Should we throw a dance party?

原句 *Shall we set about some revels?*

中文 我們要不要來辦一場舞會？

---

894. govern *(vt.)* , *(vi.)* 統治，管理

---

895. torso *(n.)* 軀幹

英文 That governs the torso and heart.

原句 *That's sides and heart.*

中文 那掌管軀幹和心。

| **896.** | obnoxious *(adj.)* 討厭的，難聞的 |

| **897.** | get the job done *(ph.)* 把事情完成 |

英文 Be loud and obnoxious. Do whatever it takes, just get the job done.

原句 *Be clamorous, and leap all civil bounds, rather than make unprofited return.*

中文 寧可吵鬧失禮，也不要徒勞無功。

| **898.** | hypothetically *(adv.)* 假設地，假定地 |

英文 Let's say hypothetically that I do get a chance to speak with her, my lord. What do I do then?

原句 *Say I do speak with her, my lord, what then?*

中文 假如我能和她交談，大人，接下來要怎麼做？

| **899.** | succeed *(vt.)* 接替，繼承；*(vi.)* 成功，繼任，繼承 |

900. assignment (*n.*) 任務，作業，分配，指派

英文 If you succeed at this assignment, I'll reward you well. My whole fortune will be yours.

原句 *Prosper well in this, and thou shalt live as freely as thy lord, to call his fortunes thine.*

中文 假如你把這件事辦好，我會好好獎賞你，我的財產也都是你的，

● **track** *138*

901. signpost *(n.)* 路標，指示牌

英文 He says he'll stand at your door like a signpost until he speaks to you.

原句 *He says he'll stand at your door like a sheriff's post, and be the supporter to a bench, but he'll speak with you.*

中文 他說他會像指示牌一樣站在門口等妳，直到妳跟他說話。

902. breastfeed *(vt.)* 用母乳餵養；*(vi.)* 哺乳

英文 He looks like he just recently stopped breastfeeding.

原句 *One would think his mother's milk were scarce out of him.*

中文 他看起來像最近才斷奶。

903. veil *(vt.)* 以面紗遮掩，掩飾，遮蓋；*(vi.)* 戴面紗；*(n.)* 面紗，面罩，帷幕，遮蔽物

英文 Give me my veil.

原句 *Give me my veil.*

中文 把面紗給我。

904. rudeness *(n.)* 無禮貌，粗野，未加工

英文 I'm very sensitive, and even the smallest bit of rudeness hurts my feelings.

原句 *I am very comptible, even to the least sinister usage.*

中文 我非常敏感，一點點粗魯無禮的行為就會讓我感到難過。

---

905. too bad *(ph.)* 遺憾的

---

906. poetic *(adj.)* 詩的，詩人的，充滿詩意的；*(n.)* 詩學

英文 That's too bad, because I spent a long time memorizing it, and it's poetic.

原句 *Alas, I took great pains to study it, and 'tis poetical.*

中文 太遺憾了，我可是花很多時間記下來的，而且相當詩意。

---

907. passage *(n.)* 通過，通路，一段文章，一節樂曲

---

908. scripture *(n.)* 經典，經文，聖典

---

909. sermon *(n.)* 布道，說教

英文 Where's the passage of holy scripture that you're basing your sermon on?

原句 *Where lies your text?*

中文 妳的經文出於何處？

---

910. paid *(adj.)* 有薪金的，已付的，付清的

英文 I'm not a paid messenger, my lady. Keep your money.

原句 *I am no fee'd post, lady. Keep your purse.*

中文 我不是個接受酬勞的使者，小姐，請妳把錢收起來。

● track *139*

| 911. | salty *(adj.)* 鹹的，有鹽分的，鹹味濃的 |

| 912. | all over again *(ph.)* 從頭再一次 |

英文 She's been drowned in salty sea water, and now my salty tears are about to drown her memory all over again.

原句 *She is drowned already, sir, with salt water, though I seem to drown her remembrance again with more.*

中文 她淹沒在海裏，現在我的淚水會再次淹沒對她的懷念。

| 913. | cause...trouble *(ph.)* 給……帶來麻煩 |

英文 Oh, Antonio, I'm sorry I caused you so much trouble.

原句 *O good Antonio, forgive me your trouble.*

中文 啊，安東尼歐，很抱歉給你帶來麻煩。

● track *140*

| 914. | bend over *(ph.)* 俯身，折彎 |

915. whoever *(pron.)* 無論誰，到底是誰，隨便哪個人

英文 If it's worth bending over to pick up, there it is on the ground, where you can see it. If not, whoever finds it can have it.

原句 *If it be worth stooping for, there it lies in your eye. If not, be it his that finds it.*

中文 如果那值得你彎下腰撿起，那麼就在你眼前的地上；否則，就隨便誰去撿。

真的在第十二夜首演

　　《第十二夜》的首演也確實在第十二夜，因為有一本書名為《第十二夜的首夜》（First Night of twelfth Nights），內容即是在描述該劇的首演。書中相信莎士比亞是奉皇室之命，因應義大利伯西諾公爵（Duke of Bracciao）、奧西諾（Don Virginio Orsino）造訪英國，而寫下這個劇本，並在1600年的聖誕節後第十二夜（也就是隔年的1月6日）演出。但公爵來訪的消息在12月26日才傳至英國，若書中所言屬實，那就表示作者在短短的十一、二天之內就寫好劇本，演員也都熟記台詞並完成演出。

916. delude (vt.) 欺騙，哄騙，迷惑

英文 And she's deluded enough to be in love with me.

原句 *And she, mistaken, seems to dote on me.*

中文 而她卻陰錯陽差愛上我。

第二幕
第三景

● track 141

917. consist of (ph.) 由……構成

918. booze (vi.) 暴飲，痛飲；(n.) 酒，含有酒精的飲料，酒宴

英文 That's what they say, but I think life consists of food and booze.

原句 *Faith, so they say, but I think it rather consists of eating and drinking.*

中文 沒錯，據說是這樣的。不過，我認為人生不外乎就是吃吃喝喝。

919. racket (vi.) , (n.) 喧嚷，大聲吵鬧

英文 You're making a terrible racket out here!

原句 *What a caterwauling do you keep here!*

中文 你現在是在製造喧鬧！

920. out of tune *(ph.)* 音高或調子不正確，不協調

英文 That's out of tune, sir.

原句 *Out o' tune, sir.*

中文 先生，你唱走音了。

921. duel *(vi.)* , *(n.)* 決鬥

922. on one's behalf *(ph.)* 代表……人

英文 I'll write a letter challenging him to a duel on your behalf.

原句 *I'll write thee a challenge.*

中文 我幫你寫信去向他挑戰。

923. rash *(adj.)* 輕率的，急躁的，魯莽的；*(n.)* 疹，疹子

英文 Dear Sir Toby, don't do anything rash tonight.

原句 *Sweet Sir Toby, be patient for tonight.*

中文 親愛的陶貝爵士，今晚行事不要衝動。

924. persuade *(vt.)* 說服，勸服，使某人相信；*(vi.)* 被說服

英文 If I can't persuade your niece to marry me, I'm going to be in some serious financial trouble.

原句 *If I cannot recover your niece, I am a foul way out.*

中文 假如不能娶妳的姪女，我可要大大地破財了。

●track *142*

---

925. bittersweet *(adj.)* 苦樂參半的；*(n.)* 又苦又甜的東西

英文 If you ever fall in love and feel the bittersweet pain it brings, think of me.

原句 *If ever thou shalt love, in the sweet pangs of it remember me.*

中文 假如你戀愛了，體會到苦樂交集的感覺時，請記起我。

---

926. be able to *(ph.)* 能夠

英文 So find someone younger to love, or you won't be able to maintain your feelings for a long time.

原句 *Then let thy love be younger than thyself, or thy affection cannot hold the bent.*

中文 因此你要找比你年輕的情人，不然你的感情就不維持久遠。

---

927. the moment *(ph.)* 一⋯⋯ (就)

---

928. about to *(ph.)* 即將

英文 Women are like roses; the moment their beauty is in full bloom, it's about to decay.

原句 *For women are as roses, whose fair flower being once displayed, doth fall that very hour.*

中文 女人就像玫瑰，美麗的花朵盛開之後，就要凋謝了。

929. inherit *(vt.)* 繼承；*(vi.)* 成為繼承人

930. value *(vt.)* 估價，評價，重視；*(n.)* 重要性，價值，價值觀

英文 The wealth she's inherited isn't what makes me value her.

原句 *The parts that fortune hath bestowed upon her, tell her, I hold as giddily as fortune*

中文 她繼承的財富，不是我珍惜她的原因。

931. intense *(adj.)* 強烈的，極度的，熱切的

英文 No woman is strong enough to put up with the kind of intense passion I feel.

原句 *There is no woman's sides can bide the beating of so strong a passion as love doth give my heart.*

中文 沒有女人的心夠強壯，能承受我感受到的強烈愛情。

第一幕
第五景

●track *143*

932. thrilled *(adj.)* 非常興奮的，極為激動的

英文 I'll be thrilled.

原句 *I would exult, man.*

中文 我好高興！

933. be fond of *(ph.)* 喜歡，愛好

英文 Maria once told me Olivia was fond of me.

原句 *Maria once told me she did affect me.*

中文 瑪麗雅有一次告訴我奧莉維亞喜歡我。

934. reach out *(ph.)* 伸手

935. stern *(adj.)* 嚴格的，苛刻的，堅定的

英文 I reach out my hand to him like this, giving him a stern look instead of my usual friendly smile

原句 *I extend my hand to him thus, quenching my familiar smile with an austere regard of control*

中文 我這樣向他伸出手，收起日常的和善笑容，給他一個嚴厲的眼光。

936. pretentious *(adj.)* 做作的，自命不凡的，炫耀的

937. riddle *(n.)* 謎語，謎一般的人，難題

英文 What a pretentious riddle!

原句 *A fustian riddle!*

中文 好一個浮誇的謎語！

938. dowry *(n.)* 嫁妝，天賦，天資

939. except for *(ph.)* 除了……以外

英文 And I wouldn't ask for any dowry except for her to play another trick like this one.

原句 *And ask no other dowry with her but such another jest.*

中文 我不要她的嫁妝，只要她再開一次這樣的玩笑。

940. sneaky *(adj.)* 鬼鬼祟祟的，暗中的

英文 I'd follow you to the gates of Hell, you sneaky devil!

原句 *To the gates of Tartar, thou most excellent devil of wit!*

中文 我會跟你到地獄的門口，你這機詐的惡魔。

第三幕
第一景

●track *144*

941. clergyman *(n.)* 神職人員，牧師，教士

英文 Are you a clergyman?

原句 *Art thou a churchman?*

中文 你是神職人員嗎？

942. care about *(ph.)* 關心，擔心，在乎

英文 I bet you're a happy fellow who doesn't care about anything.

原句 *I warrant thou art a merry fellow and carest for nothing.*

中文 我敢說你是個快樂的人，內心沒任何掛念。

943. foolishness *(n.)* 愚蠢，愚笨

944. all over the world *(ph.)* 全世界，世界各地，
遍及全世界

英文 Foolishness is all over the world, just like sunshine.

原句 *Foolery, sir, does walk about the orb like the sun.*

中文 愚蠢像陽光一樣，到處都有。

945. downhill *(adj.)* 下坡的；*(adv.)* 下坡地；
(n.) 向下，向坡下

946. pass for *(ph.)* 被認為是，誤認為是

947. humility *(n.)* 謙卑，謙遜

948. compliment *(vt.)* , *(n.)* 讚美，恭維，祝賀

英文 The world's gone downhill since fake humility started
passing for compliments.

原句 *'Twas never merry world since lowly feigning was
call'd compliment.*

中文 虛假的謙遜一旦被認為是種讚美，世界就要變得不好
了。

949. wear one' heart on one' sleeve *(ph.)* 流露出感情，
對某人示愛

英文 I'm wearing my heart on my sleeve, and I can't hide
my feelings.

原句 *A cypress, not a bosom, hideth my heart.*

中文 我對你吐露了感情，無法再隱藏了。

950. hide *(vt.)* 隱藏，隱瞞，掩蔽；*(vi.)* 躲藏，隱藏；
(n.) 隱密場所

英文 A murderer can hide his guilt longer than someone in love can hide her love.

原句 *A murderous guilt shows not itself more soon than love that would seem hid.*

中文 愛情比謀殺更快被洩露。

兩種願望與欲望

　　《第十二夜》整齣劇充斥著願望與欲望的展現。其中欲望的表現形式分為兩種：一種即以四位男女主角為中心的主要情節，著眼於浪漫愛情的奉獻與追求；另一種則是以配角等人為主的次情節線，著眼於名利與私慾的渴望。後者是僅止於表面利益的膚淺情感，與前者至高無上的浪漫愛情實有很大的差異。

● track 145

951. orchard (*n.*) 果園

英文 I saw it in the orchard.

原句 *I saw 't i' the orchard.*

中文 我在果園裏看見的。

952. airtight (*adj.*) 密閉的，無懈可擊的

953. argument (*n.*) 爭吵，辯論，論點

英文 I'll prove it with airtight evidence and logical arguments.

原句 *I will prove it legitimate, sir, upon the oaths of judgment and reason.*

中文 我會以無懈可擊的證據和合理的論點來證明。

● track 146

954. inconvenience (*vt.*) 給……造成不便；(*n.*) 麻煩，打擾，不便之處

955. nag *(vt.)* 使煩惱，跟……糾纏不休；*(vi.)* 不斷嘮叨，責罵不休；*(n.)* 好嘮叨的人

英文 I really didn't want to inconvenience you. But since you seem to enjoy helping me, I won't nag you to stop any more.

原句 *I would not by my will have troubled you; but, since you make your pleasure of your pains, I will no further chide you.*

中文 我真的不願意麻煩你，不過既然你樂在其中，我就不再嘮叨了。

956. conspicuous *(adj.)* 顯眼的，引人注意的

英文 Then don't make yourself too conspicuous.

原句 *Do not then walk too open.*

中文 你不要讓自己太引人注意。

第三幕
第四景

●track *147*

957. possess *(vt.)* 擁有，具有，掌握

英文 He's coming, madam; but he's acting very strangely. He must be possessed by the devil.

原句 *He's coming, madam; but in very strange manner. He is sure possessed, madam.*

中文 他要來了，小姐；不過他表現得很奇怪，一定是被魔鬼附身了。

---

958. nonsense *(n.)* 胡說，胡鬧，無價值的東西

英文 Why, what's the matter with him? Is he talking nonsense?

原句 *Why, what's the matter? Does he rave?*

中文 為何？他怎麼了？他會亂説話嗎？

---

959. sent for *(ph.)* 派人去請，讓人去取

---

960. occasion *(n.)* 場合，時刻，時機

英文 Why are you smiling? I sent for you about a sad occasion.

原句 *Smilest thou? I sent for thee upon a sad occasion.*

中文 你為什麼在笑？我派人找你來是為了一件悲傷的事。

---

961. on purpose *(ph.)* 故意地，為了

英文 She's sending him to me on purpose, so I can be rude to him just like she said in the letter.

原句 *She sends him on purpose that I may appear stubborn to him, for she incites me to that in the letter.*

中文 她刻意派他來，這樣我就會對他無禮，就像她在信裏説的。

---

962. fulfillment *(n.)* 完成，實現，滿足，成就

英文 Nothing can come between me and the fulfillment of all my hopes.

原句 *Nothing that can be can come between me and the*

full prospect of my hopes.

中文 沒有任何事情能夠阻擋我實現我的希望。

---

963. take to heart *(ph.)* 認真關注，對……想不開

---

964. prank *(vi.)* , *(n.)* 胡鬧，惡作劇

---

965. play the role *(ph.)* 扮演角色

英文 He's really taken this prank to heart. He's playing the role perfectly.

原句 *His very genius hath taken the infection of the device, man.*

中文 他對這個惡作劇很投入，完美地扮演他的角色。

---

966. divulge *(vt.)* 洩露；暴露

英文 No, follow him now, before he divulges the prank and ruins everything.

原句 *Nay, pursue him now, lest the device take air and taint.*

中文 不能這樣，現在就跟著他，避免他洩露並毀了這場惡作劇。

---

967. serve as *(ph.)* 有……的效果，當作……用

---

968. go-between *(n.)* 媒介者，中間人，居間調停

---

969. confirm *(vt.)* 證實，確認，批准

英文 The fact that he serves as a go-between for his lord and my niece confirms this.

原句 *His employment between his lord and my niece confirms no less.*

中文 他充當他主人的中間人，我的姪女已經證明這一點。

---

970. insignificant *(adj.)* 地位低微的，無足輕重的，無意義

英文 He realizes it's so insignificant that it's not worth talking about.

原句 *He finds that now scarce to be worth talking of.*

中文 他發現那實在是微不足道。

---

971. cap *(n.)* 無邊便帽，制服帽

英文 I recognize your face perfectly, even without a sailor's cap on your head

原句 *I know your favor well, though now you have no sea-cap on your head.*

中文 我熟識你的臉孔，雖然你現在沒有戴航海的帽子。

---

972. in a sense *(ph.)* 在某種意義上

英文 I know my brother is still alive in a sense, since I see him whenever I look in the mirror.

原句 *I my brother know yet living in my glass.*

中文 我知道我哥哥某種意義上是活著的，因為我照鏡子時會從鏡子裡看到他 (因為她和哥哥是雙胞胎)。

973. pointless *(adj.)* 無意義的，不尖的，不得要領的

974. clumsy *(adj.)* 笨拙的，手腳不靈活，不得體的

975. come up with *(ph.)* 想出，提供，趕上

英文 Come with me to my house. I'll tell you about all the pointless, clumsy pranks this thug uncle of mine has come up with, so that you can laugh at this one.

原句 *Go with me to my house, and hear thou there how many fruitless pranks this ruffian hath botched up, that thou thereby mayst smile at this.*

中文 跟我回家，我會告訴你我叔叔家那個壞蛋所策畫的荒唐計謀，你就可以對這件事一笑置之。

976. impudent *(adj.)* 厚顏無恥的，放肆的，粗魯的

977. ounce *(n.)* 盎司，(常用於否定句) 一點點，少量

英文 What? No. Because then I'd have to shed an ounce or two of your impudent blood.

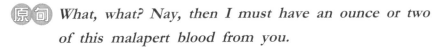

原句 *What, what? Nay, then I must have an ounce or two of this malapert blood from you.*

中文 什麼？不！那麼我就只好讓你流出一些傲慢的血。

---

978. keep on *(ph.)* 繼續

英文 If this is a dream, let me keep on sleeping!

原句 *If it be thus to dream, still let me sleep!*

中文 假如這是在作夢，請別叫醒我！

第四幕
第一景

● track *149*

---

979. shut up *(ph.)* 關閉，監禁，住口

英文 They've shut me up here in horrible darkness.

原句 *They have laid me here in hideous darkness.*

中文 他們把我關在這個黑暗的地方。

---

980. commonsense *(adj.)* 常識的

英文 Ask me any commonsense question.

原句 *Make the trial of it in any constant question.*

中文 隨便問我一般常識的問題。

---

981. inhabit *(vt.)* 居住於，棲息於，占據

英文 That our grandmother's soul could end up inhabiting a bird.

原句 *That the soul of our grandam might haply inhabit a bird.*

中文 我們祖母的靈魂可能棲息在鳥的身體裏。

982. belief *(n.)* 相信，信念，信仰

英文 I respect the soul very much, so I disagree with his belief.

原句 *I think nobly of the soul, and no way approve his opinion.*

中文 因為我對靈魂非常尊重，所以無法同意他的看法。

983. babbling *(adj.)* 胡說的；*(n.)* 胡說

英文 Try to sleep, and stop your pointless babbling.

原句 *Endeavor thyself to sleep, and leave thy vain bibble-babble.*

中文 你設法睡著，不要再胡說八道。

愛情的夢幻之地

《第十二夜》的背景是設定發生在伊利里亞（Illyria）的故事，該字的本義有幻想、幻影之意。這預設了在這種夢幻之處愛情會有千變萬化的可能性，而正是因為沈溺在這樣一個充滿幻想、幻象的國度裡，每一個人才可以盡力去追求和抓住每一段可能的愛情，因此劇中的每一個人都在這樣充滿可能性的環境，汲汲營營地尋找自己的愛情美夢並努力讓美夢成真。

第四幕
第三景

●track *150*

| **984.** | feel *(vt.)* 摸，觸，感覺，認為；*(vi.)* 有感覺，覺得，摸索；*(n.)* 觸覺，手感 |

| **985.** | confused *(adj.)* 混亂的，亂七八糟的，困惑的 |

英文 I can feel and see this pearl she gave me. I may be dazed and confused, but I'm not insane.

原句 *This pearl she gave me, I do feel't and see't; and though 'tis wonder that enwraps me thus, yet't is not madness.*

中文 我可以摸得到她送給我的珍珠，我或許是被弄糊塗而已，並沒有發瘋。

| **986.** | intention *(n.)* 意圖，意向，含義 |

| **987.** | holy *(adj.)* 神聖的，至善的 |

| **988.** | chapel *(n.)* 小教堂 |

| **989.** | make a vow *(ph.)* 發誓 |

英文 If your intentions toward me are honorable, come with me and this holy man into the chapel over there, where you can soothe all my worries by making your marriage vow to me.

原句 *If you mean well, now go with me and with this holy man into the Chantry by; there, before him, and underneath that consecrated roof, plight me the full assurance of your faith; that my most jealous and too doubtful soul may live at peace.*

中文 假如你有誠心，就和我以及這位牧師到附近教堂，在他的面前宣告你的誓言，讓我憂慮的心得到平靜。

第五幕
第一景

● track *151*

---

990. rescue *(vt.)* , *(n.)* 援救，營救

---

991. ungrateful *(adj.)* 不感激的，忘恩負義的，不領情的

英文 I rescued that ungrateful boy next to you from drowning.

原句 *That most ingrateful boy there by your side, from the rude sea's enraged and foamy mouth did I redeem.*

中文 我從海裏拯救了，那個站在你旁邊忘恩負義的青年。

---

992. repulsive *(adj.)* 使人反感的，令人厭惡的，可憎的

---

993. scream *(vt.)* 尖叫，放聲大哭，放聲大笑；
(vi.) 尖叫著說；*(n.)* 尖叫，尖銳刺耳的聲音

英文 If what you have to say is anything like what you used to say, it'll be as repulsive to my ears as wild screams after listening to beautiful music.

原句 *If it be aught to the old tune, my lord, it is as fat and fulsome to mine ear as howling after music.*

中文 假如你還要說那些你一直在說的老調，我聽了會很反感，就好像欣賞美妙的音樂後聽到野蠻的吼叫。

---

994. join in *(ph.)* 參加

995. eternal *(adj.)* 永久的，無窮的，不朽的

996. bond *(n.)* 結合力，聯繫，公債

997. matrimony *(n.)* 婚姻，夫婦關係，婚姻生活

英文 They were joined in an eternal bond of love and matrimony, and it was confirmed by a holy kiss and an exchange of rings.

原句 *A contract of eternal bond of love, confirmed by mutual joinder of yourhands, attested by the holy close of lips, strengthened by interchangement of your rings.*

中文 他們結下永世愛情的盟約，而且親吻過彼此、交換過戒指。

998. mole *(n.)* 痣，鼴鼠，錢鼠

英文 My father had a mole on his forehead.

原句 *My father had a mole upon his brow.*

中文 我爸爸的額頭上有一顆痣。

999. miraculous *(adj.)* 神奇的，超自然的，奇蹟般的

英文 Please don't let squabbles ruin this beautiful and miraculous moment.

原句 *Let no quarrel nor no brawl to come taint the condition of this present hour.*

中文 請不要讓爭吵破壞眼前的好事。

1000. thrust upon *(ph.)* 把某事強加於某人

英文 Some are born great, some achieve greatness, and some have greatness thrust upon them.

原句 *Some are born great, some achieve greatness, and some have greatness thrown upon them.*

中文 有些人天生高貴，有些人贏得尊貴，有些人則是尊貴自然相加於身。

永續圖書
線上購物網

www.foreverbooks.com.tw

◆ 加入會員即享活動及會員折扣。

◆ 每月均有優惠活動，期期不同。

◆ 新加入會員三天內訂購書籍不限本數金額，

即贈送精選書籍一本。（依網站標示為主）

專業圖書發行、書局經銷、圖書出版

永續圖書總代理：

五觀藝術出版社、培育文化、棋茵出版社、大拓文化、讀
品文化、雅典文化、知音人文化、手藝家出版社、璞申文
化、智學堂文化、語言鳥文化

活動期內，永續圖書將保留變更或終止該活動之權利及最終決定權。

跟莎士比亞一學就會的1000單字

雅致風靡　典藏文化

親愛的顧客您好，感謝您購買這本書。

為了提供您更好的服務品質，煩請填寫下列回函資料，您的支持是我們最大的動力。

您可以選擇傳真、掃描或用本公司準備的免郵回函寄回，謝謝。

姓名：	性別：	□男　　□女
出生日期：　　年　　月　　日　電話：		
學歷：	職業：	□男　　□女
E-mail：		
地址：□□□		
從何得知本書消息：□逛書店　□朋友推薦　□DM廣告　□網路雜誌		
購買本書動機：□封面　□書名　□排版　□內容　□價格便宜		
你對本書的意見： 內容：□滿意□尚可□待改進　　編輯：□滿意□尚可□待改進 封面：□滿意□尚可□待改進　　定價：□滿意□尚可□待改進		
其他建議：		

剪下後傳真、掃描或寄回至「221 03新北市汐止區大同路3段194號9樓之1雅典文化收」

總經銷：永續圖書有限公司

永續圖書線上購物網
www.foreverbooks.com.tw

您可以使用以下方式將回函寄回。

您的回覆，是我們進步的最大動力，謝謝。

① 使用本公司準備的免郵回函寄回。

② 傳真電話：（02）8647-3660

③ 掃描圖檔寄到電子信箱：

yungjiuh@ms45.hinet.net

沿此線對折後寄回，謝謝。

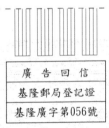

廣 告 回 信
基隆郵局登記證
基隆廣字第056號

2 2 1 0 3

 雅典文化事業有限公司　收
新北市汐止區大同路三段194號9樓之1

雅致風靡　典藏文化